# TRACKERS

## BOOK TWO

## SHANTORIAN

# PATRICK CARMAN

# TRACKERS

## BOOK TWO
## SHANTORIAN

SCHOLASTIC INC.
New York Toronto London Auckland
Sydney Mexico City New Delhi Hong Kong

PC STUDIO

ISBN 978-0-545-41455-5

Copyright © 2011 by Patrick Carman.
All rights reserved. Published by Scholastic Inc.
SCHOLASTIC and associated logos are trademarks
and/or registered trademarks of Scholastic Inc.

12 11 10 9 8 7 6 5 4 3 2 1          11 12 13 14 15 16/0

Printed in the U.S.A.          40

First Scholastic paperback printing, October 2011

The text was set in Adobe Garamond Pro.
Book design by Christopher Stengel

**AGENT REPORT:** Classified.
**SECURITY CLEARANCE:** RED-2, Supermax personnel ONLY.
**SUBJECT:** Trackers' entry into underground organization ISD.

*File Update*

*Day one yielded significant progress with subject Adam Henderson. Report from interrogation rooms 2, 3, and 4 far less encouraging. No one else is talking. The rest of Henderson's team—Lewis, Finn, and Emily— remain unresponsive to questions. Henderson is telling these events, no one else. Has he scared the others into silence, or do they trust him to get every last detail right? For now there is no one to confirm Adam's version of events.*

*Adam Henderson presents an unusual interrogation challenge. He appears to have a photographic memory, repeating conversations he's had verbatim, describing locations in perfect detail. He speaks as if he's building an elaborate story, one block at a time. Is he lying? Almost certainly. But he has piles of evidence hidden away in his mind, and videos, lots of them, which he will only locate and open on his terms. So far he has revealed nine videos, but he claims to have more.*

*Primary data capture during first stage of interrogation:*

- *National banks breached, billions remain unaccounted for. Adam Henderson has shown me nothing that would prove his innocence. He is brilliant, no doubt, but sooner or later he will make a mistake.*
- *Adam Henderson's collaborators, the Trackers, are the other individuals we have in custody: Lewis Booker (room 2), Emily Chance (room 3), and James "Finn" Durant (room 4). Ms. Chance's resolve is strong, Mr. Durant is perpetually asleep, and Mr. Booker is holding but nervous, the most likely to break. I'll put him in with Adam shortly.*
- *Henderson casts the Trackers as innocent teens playing hi-tech spy games. These games, or field tests, led two individuals — Lazlo and Zara — to lure the Trackers into a secret organization called ISD (the Internet Security Directive). According to Henderson, his involvement in looting billions from banks was not a theft, but a test to gain entry into the secret organization.*
- *No knowledge of ISD is attainable from our database search. Either ISD is a lie, created by Henderson to cover his tracks, or ISD has a government security level of RED-3 (highly unlikely, as RED-3, my colleagues will note, is reserved for top*

level international spy activity. Even I don't have RED-3 clearance).

- Henderson would have us believe his surveillance "gadgets" were used by ISD in an effort to hunt down someone we are all aware of: Shantorian, the most notorious computer hacker on file.

- This segment of Henderson's story is confirmed: Shantorian is extremely dangerous, a known threat to world security with a meaningful price on his head. Whoever brings him in, dead or alive, receives the largest reward in criminal case history: $10,000,000.

- Reward or no reward, a two-year hunt has produced exactly zero leads of consequence. Shantorian is many things: powerful, dangerous, elusive, unpredictable. His command of the Internet is legendary. When he strikes, it is often catastrophic.

- Rumors persist of Shantorian's ability to shut down the Internet entirely, using the celebrated Raymond disk. Adam Henderson claims to have had this device in his possession, though now, he insists, it is in the hands of ISD.

- If Henderson is to be believed, Lazlo is the leader of ISD, Zara the brilliant protégé.

- Zara, Henderson claims, is young like the Trackers, and mysterious. Her last name is not known.

- Do Zara and Lazlo exist outside of Adam's dazzling imagination? Apparently so. I've seen them both.

- *We continue to risk holding the Trackers without the consent of legal guardians. As soon as we bring in the parents, everything gets more complicated. The only reason we can do this is that world security is at stake...and time is running out.*
- *As I begin round two of my interrogation, I know three things:*

    1) *Billions are still missing.*
    2) *Adam Henderson is lying to me.*
    3) *I will break him.*

*Subject is alert. Almost too alert, it seems to me. He's caught his second wind. Multiple recording devices initiated. Agents standing by at rooms 2, 3, and 4. Top-level officials from Washington have arrived, watching these proceedings from behind mirrored glass to my left.*

*It's go time.*

**Your energy surprises even me, Adam.**

It shouldn't. I've pulled a lot of all-nighters. But if you're too tired to go on, I can wait. Or maybe you want to send in the henchmen from behind the double glass.

**I've done plenty of twenty-four-hour stakeouts. Trust me, I can go a lot longer than you can.**

Wanna bet?

**Let's talk about ISD.**

Not until I see Finn. That was our deal.

**We didn't have a deal — *you* had a demand. I'm telling you no.**

I don't like you.

**Understood. But, Adam, you don't want to deal with my superiors. That's an interview I wouldn't wish on my worst enemy. You're in deep. Nothing you've said convinces me you didn't hack into these banks. You need to tell me about ISD.**

Two cans of Red Bull, a Snickers, and Finn. That's my final offer.

**Five minutes with *Lewis* and a glass of water.**

And the Snickers bar.

**Done.**

*I made the call, poured the glass of water, and waited until the door opened.*

*Lewis Booker was cuffed to the leg of the metal table at 01:54.*

*Lieutenant Marks stood at the ready, should anything go wrong. The candy bar arrived and was presented to Adam.*

**Clock's ticking, gentlemen. You've got five minutes.**

> AH: How are you holding up?

> LB: Okay, I guess. They keep asking the same questions and I keep giving the same answer, like we agreed.

AH: And the answer is?

LB: Ask Adam Henderson.

AH: Good. Have you seen Emily or Finn?

LB: Nope. Just four walls, a table, and a chair. I fell asleep for a while....Listen, Adam, I'm not sure how much longer I can do this.

AH: I'm getting close. I've got it all dialed in, but it takes time. There's a lot to tell.

LB: Right, okay. My lips are sealed.

AH: Here, take this. I got it for you. You're sure you haven't said *anything*? Not a word?

LB: I'm sure. Hurry up, okay?

*Adam slid the Snickers bar across the table and Lewis took it. They have two more minutes, but it's clear they have nothing else to say. Adam is running this train right off a cliff all by himself. Lieutenant Marks uncuffed Lewis and returned him to room 2.*

**Lewis Booker is lying to you. He's already told us plenty. So are the rest of your friends. Funny, your stories don't line up so well.**

I hate to be the one to break it to you, because I know how it will hurt your ego, but Lewis hasn't said a word and you know it.

**That's where you're wrong.**

Really? Then why'd he take the Snickers bar?

**What does a candy bar have to do with anything?**

Before you dragged us all in here I devised a few plans of my own, see? I gave a few instructions about what to do if we were hauled into a situation just like this one. One of them was pretty simple: If I see you and I offer you something, only take it if the answer you're giving is true. If it's not, refuse. I asked Lewis if he'd said anything and he said no. He took the Snickers bar, which I'd like back since I'm craving one of those after-midnight sugar rushes, but the fact is, he took it.

**Maybe he's lying to you. Ever think of that?**

Nope, never crossed my mind. You wanna know why? Because I know my friends better than you obviously know yours.

Lewis never lies. *Ever.* It's not in his nature to lie, at least not to me or the rest of us. Maybe you don't have friends like that. I can see how that might be the case, being in the line of work you're in: a lot of conniving, a lot of jockeying for position, that sort of thing. It's not like that with us. We don't lie to each other.

And since we're on the subject of my friends, thank you for reading this situation like I expected you to. I asked for Finn, so I knew you wouldn't give me Finn. You figured I had to see him most, that I might crack under the pressure if I didn't see the one guy I had to see. News flash: I just saw the one guy I needed to see. Lewis is the nervous one. He's the one who would have buckled, but he's holding strong. That's all I needed to know. Finn and Emily? Good luck. Those guys won't talk unless you torture them, and last time I checked, this isn't the Middle Ages.

**Tell me about ISD right now, or so help me I will leave this room and never come back. You want to start over? That's your problem. We're ten hours in and I'm a reasonable person. The guy you're going to get if I leave this room is my boss. *Not* a reasonable person. Especially at two in the morning.**

*Adam is staring at the door, the wheels turning in his head. If he calls my bluff the case will grind to a halt. There is no one else. I'm the best we've got. And he's right that none of his friends are talking.*

The ISD training facility was everything a supergeek could hope for, and the cover was perfect: an expensive summer camp for gifted kids located outside the city in a converted hangar. In fact, that's what Lazlo called it when he sold the idea to my parents. I remember Lazlo's words exactly, because I hung on every word, hoping my parents would go for it:

"We've converted one of the first-generation Boeing airplane hangars," he said. "Amazing facility. And Microsoft has contributed mightily to our success as a program. Adam is one of our brightest stars, so naturally he'd attend the camp on a full scholarship."

Lazlo could really sell, no doubt about it. What parent could say no to Boeing (the largest airplane maker in the world), Microsoft (the most powerful company in the world), and three weeks of intensive training on the coolest new computer applications? My parents were melting under the spell of Lazlo's untraceable international accent. But Lazlo didn't stop there.

"We're aware of Adam's association with a group of friends who test his equipment. Not to be to blunt, Mr. and Mrs. Henderson, but quite frankly they're not at the same level Adam is. Then again, who is? However, they have played an important role in testing a lot of Adam's more promising inventions. This is very unusual, in fact we've never done it before, but we'd like to offer full scholarships to them as well, so Adam will have everything he needs to—how shall we say?—take things to the next level. I'm meeting with their parents just as soon as we conclude."

Let's just say the icing on the cake wasn't exactly necessary. My dad started one of the first computer repair shops in the world and his number one client, twenty years running, was Microsoft. He put up a good front, though.

"It will be hard to do without him at the shop for three weeks, but I think I can manage," he said. "You're sure it's completely paid for?"

Lazlo confirmed the scholarship by pulling out some surprisingly sophisticated documentation, complete with the school logo, the Microsoft stamp of approval, and several places to sign. My mom had zero reservations. It was summer, and in her opinion there was far too much idle time to begin with. Plus she was a strong proponent of summer camps in general, though she'd never managed to convince me to attend one. Before Lazlo could get the pen out of his suit pocket, she was signing with her own pen, fresh off of edits from the Magellan book she was writing.

"Wow, Mom, I hadn't realized how excited you were to get rid of me," I said. I was only half joking.

"Do like the explorers and live a little" was all she said, but her look told me more. For all her solitude as a writer and researcher, my mom would miss me.

I was officially attending TechBase10, a camp that didn't exist, didn't actually charge five thousand dollars per student, and didn't have the endorsement of Microsoft or Boeing.

**When you tell a lie, you don't mess around.**

Point taken. But try to see it from my perspective. This was an opportunity to catch the most wanted cybercriminal in the world. ISD wanted to use my inventions, my brain, and my team to do something really important. I believed it was the right thing to do, given the circumstances.

**Why not simply tell your parents what you were doing?**

They hadn't gone through the testing we had. They hadn't earned their way into ISD. And let's be honest — my parents, superspies? We're talking about a bookworm and a computer nerd. I love 'em to death, but they didn't exactly match the ISD profile.

Lazlo needed complete secrecy, and he needed young, talented agents. I understood that and, actually, agreed with it. I think my parents would have freaked if they'd known what we were doing. ISD's cover could have been blown, putting years of work at risk.

**So you were undercover secret agents, fighting the good fight, like in the movies. I can understand how someone of your generation might fall for that.**

So you believe me, then?

**No. I still think you're making this up as you go. But if there ever was a camp called TechBase10 where they**

**tricked kids into thinking they were spies, I'm sure you'd fall for it.**

I mentioned the part about how I don't like you already, but just so there's no confusion, now I like you even less.

**So you fooled your parents, or Lazlo did, and I assume all the other parents went along as well.**

How could they refuse? TechBase10 had a legitimate Web site, Lazlo was a perfect front man, and we weren't going to the Ukraine. Heck, the camp was forty-five minutes away. They could call us if they wanted. The only sketchy part was when we were all dropped off.

Lazlo didn't go to quite as much trouble preparing the hangar as he did selling the idea of it to our parents. There was a sign over the main door—TechBase10—but other than that, the place looked deserted. Four dads, one mom, and four teenagers stood in front of the monstrous hangar as a tumbleweed drifted by. And then Zara appeared.

"Welcome to the future; you're the first to arrive" was her introduction. She was confident, beautiful, smart, and totally at ease. She introduced herself to the parents, including a little tidbit about each of them, things that were personal but not *too* personal. Shaking Mr. Chance's hand she gushed, "I *love* remote control airplanes. Have you flown the RTF Ambassador? It screams."

Emily is an RC monster truck lover, but her dad is into the flying remotes. Zara had him and all the other parents wrapped around her finger within seconds of her arrival. She talked up all the parents as she pointed to lots of outer doors without actually going inside.

"This hangar is bigger than a football field and over a hundred feet high. You can't imagine the heating bill."

Everyone laughed and felt at ease as Zara walked around the building, offering historical tidbits about Boeing "back in the day."

**She sounds like a real charmer.**

It was more than that. It was like our parents couldn't help but trust her, especially when she started gushing about *us*.

"This is my fourth year, and every year the groups get smarter," she said, looking at each of us. "But I think this year is the most talented group yet. So does Mr. Gates."

There's nothing a parent likes more than thinking some-one *else* thinks their kid is überspecial. But this whopper of a lie—that Bill Gates, the founder of Microsoft, had personally reviewed the incoming TechBase10 class and thought we were the best group ever to attend—this lie was so big it had to be true. At least that's what our parents thought.

At that point we could have been standing in front of a deserted building—which we were, for the most part—and it wouldn't have mattered. Zara captivated our parents' socks off. They were hypnotized by her awesomeness, just like me and Finn and Lewis. The only holdout was Emily, who had the look of a cat vying for territory.

Once our parents were putty in Zara's hands, she opened one of the doors leading into the hangar. It was the only door my parents would ever see opened at TechBase10.

Behind this door there was a base of operations. This was

the front of the hangar, where once there had been offices, work-rooms, and an open entry space. Those rooms remained, and Lazlo explained them: the girls' and boys' dormitories, hardware development, software programming, 3-D modeling, and networking. Each had a sign, but we didn't enter any of them. I sneaked glances at Emily, Finn, and Lewis. We all knew the truth: If our parents looked inside those rooms, they'd find old airplane parts, boxes of junk, and not much else.

Beyond the base of operations, which took up maybe ten percent of the hangar, there was the hangar itself, huge and empty.

**Draw it for me, the layout of those rooms.**

*I offered a pencil and paper. Let the record show that Adam Henderson drew the diagram opposite in the space of three minutes.*

**This drawing has the Vault on it. Are you telling me you brought it from home?**

Sure I brought the Vault. How else was I going to do surveillance for ISD? All my stuff ran from the Vault: software programs, remote feeds from the camera phones, navigation systems—*everything*. Guys like me, we build a world of hardware and software around ourselves. It's *our* world, and we understand it better than anyone else. We're comfortable there.

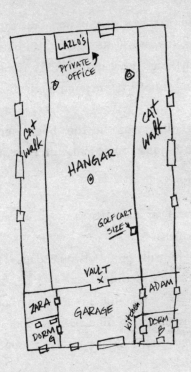

It was my idea to unhinge everything from the closet in the computer shop and load it in the shop truck. I knew I'd need it all to catch Shantorian.

Back at Henderson's Chip Shop, the Vault was just that: small, stuffy, no windows to the world outside. But here in the hangar, Lazlo had built a 20 x 20 room out of ten-foot-high chain-link fence. It looked like the venue for a high-tech cage match, with power strips and computer parts piled up in every corner.

The other parents helped unload the Vault in pieces and then, after a few more questions and some awkward hugs, they were gone. The Trackers disappeared into the hangar with Zara and Lazlo. It was just me and my dad putting the pieces of the Vault back together. I didn't trust anyone else with the higher skill of reconnecting wires and motherboards.

**So everyone else was in the back section of the hangar or had gone home, and it was just you and your dad?**

Yeah, just me and my dad. It was tough, because I knew he was excited for me.

He said, "I'm really proud of you, Adam. This is going to be the experience of a lifetime."

Maybe it was something in my expression or the vast emptiness of the hangar behind us that made the Vault feel small and insignificant. Whatever the reason, he suddenly looked concerned.

"You scared?" he asked me.

"Maybe a little," I admitted. "I think they'll expect a lot of me."

After I said those words, he took me by the shoulders and we locked eyes.

"Just do your best, that'll be more than enough."

**Must be hard lying to a dad as nice as yours.**

Technically, I didn't lie. I withheld the truth.

**Same thing, champ.**

If you're going to insult me, at least do me the courtesy of calling me Adam. Champ is what you call a four-year-old or a dog, and I'm neither.

**You don't make the rules around here, I do. *Champ*. What happened after you finished lying to your dad and he left for home?**

You're, like, zero fun.

**Just answer the question.**

We spent the next couple of hours getting the lay of the land, which was helped along by two old electric golf carts. Lewis and I took turns driving. All Finn wanted to do was ride.

I remember Finn yelling as we pulled him around by a rope on his skateboard: "This is better than the Green Lantern!" And that was saying something, because the Green Lantern is a private half-pipe heaven. The hangar was big and open, with a smooth concrete floor the size of a professional soccer field. The rope was about twelve feet long, and no matter how hard I turned, I couldn't whip Finn off his board. The guy is a real maniac on that thing.

**Where was Emily during this important work you were doing?**

There were iron beams running all over the place and crazy catwalks made of metal grating. The catwalks spanned the whole hangar, winding way up into the round top and down both sides. Emily was up there a lot at the start, looking down on the rest of the space, zooming the Trinity camera from left to right. She was in full surveillance mode from the get-go. I think it was partly because she didn't want to encounter Zara any more than she had to.

After a while we got hungry and Zara pointed us to some pizza boxes and bottles of water. I remember Finn was very depressed about the water.

"Where's the Mountain Dew? Where's the Red Bull? I can't live like this!"

He was a real crack-up when things got tense, over the top about stuff that didn't really matter.

"I wouldn't get used to 'this,'" Zara warned us. "Pizza is a one-time thing. After that, it's ramen noodles twenty-four seven."

We all looked at her, hoping she was joking, but none of us could tell for sure.

We got a look at all the rooms, starting with my private software-crunching/gadget-building zone. I'd given Lazlo a shopping list and he'd tripled my order on every front. There were crates of old cell phones, game controllers, camera parts, motherboards, and monitors. Also a massive rolling tool chest, a soldering gun, blowtorches, and jars filled with bolts and nails.

"Pretty sweet," Lewis said. "You could build some serious weaponry in here."

"I plan on it" was the answer I gave, because I was seriously jacked. Between this room and the Vault, I had enough building material and space to make a life-size robot with nine arms, removable armor, a fridge, and a microwave.

Zara had a similar room all to herself, only hers was very neat and tidy. There was a desk, a chair, beds, and a computer. Nothing else. She was a minimalist, for sure, but she knew how to sling code with the best. If this was how she rolled, I was cool with that.

When Emily realized she'd be bunking in the same room with Zara, she said, "I'd rather sleep in the same room with a chain-saw-wielding zombie."

Ouch. Kind of harsh. At least that's what the guys and I thought. But Zara was of a different mind.

"Just don't leave your dirty clothes lying around and we'll get along fine," she told Emily. "We're not going to be doing a lot of sleeping anyway. We've got work to do."

And then Zara said something that surprised us all: "Speaking of work, the sun has set. Time for our first test."

"Test?" asked Lewis. "Who said anything about a test? I thought we were already in."

"Oh, you're in," Zara replied. "But Lazlo thinks you're soft. To be fair, he includes me in that category at the moment. Shantorian is a whole different level. Lazlo says it's time we realized that."

The moment Zara said this, the lights went out, like someone had shut the breaker off. It was pitch-dark in the hangar and I was holding a slice of pizza.

"Guys, what's going on?" Emily asked. She was prepared, a mini-flashlight out and pointing at the floor.

Finn spun the wheels on his skateboard as Zara's voice came up over speakers:

"Lazlo is on the move. We need a license plate number and a state. Go!"

**How did you react?**

We had no idea there was even going to *be* a test, but I was encouraged by how quickly a plan was formed. I took up my position at the Vault, firing up monitors and handing out devices. Lewis had the Deckard for superzoom, Emily the Trinity for slow-motion capture, and Finn the standard issue Belinski because we were sure he'd break it.

Zara stayed with me in the Vault, producing two wireless receivers from a random box.

"You're going to need these," she said, nudging me aside as her fingers flew over the keyboard. Within seconds a whole new bank of surveillance images appeared. We had a feed on four remote cameras located outside the hangar. Between those and the mobile Tracker units, we had seven distinct viewpoints to choose from.

The test was crazy, totally reckless behavior from Lazlo. But it served its purpose.

It woke us up.

**Is this the part where you show me a video?**

Yes, ma'am. It's a good one.

**It better be. I can't take boring at this hour.**

You won't be disappointed.

*Adam Henderson typed furiously on the laptop we provided him with, turned it in my direction, and asked me to enter a password on the screen.*

*Note: A transcript of this video appears in Appendix L, page 131.*

23

www.trackersinterface.com

PASSWORD

# SHERMANFAIRCHILD

**I find it hard to imagine anyone could trust Lazlo after something like that.**

I know, right? Who drives their car over a golf cart when someone is in it? Strike that, since Lazlo was driving the car with a remote control! I didn't even know that was possible. We were chasing a phantom, or it was chasing us, while Lazlo slipped away.

But here's the thing: All of us were thinking like junior detectives until Lazlo nearly ran over half our crew. If you could have recorded my thoughts when we arrived at the hangar, they would have gone something like this: *We're not adults; we're still in school, for crying out loud. This is only going to get so dangerous and then—poof!—Lazlo will jump in and save us.*

**You really believed that?**

At the time, yes.

Lazlo's first test at the hangar put us all on alert: This was for real, someone could get hurt. Someone might even get killed.

"If we get anywhere near Shantorian, he won't hesitate to strike" was how Lazlo described the situation we were heading into.

There were a lot of tests like that first one in the days that followed. I think Lazlo got a kick out of devising ways to put us through our paces. Before long we were using full-size remote control cars ourselves, zip-lining from the catwalks, rappelling down the walls. I was constantly repairing gadgets while Emily and Finn tried to keep up with the growing list of busted-up golf carts, skateboards, and taillights. And the Vault was souped-up to handle more information coming in from multiple locations.

But the biggest thing we did during all those tests? We got really good at using my mobile devices. The Orville, the one with the flying camera, got its first real hard-core testing. The Trinity and Deckard units were also put through their paces, upgraded with new software patches as I jammed them full of more features.

No one loved our daily routine more than I did. We were in serious training, my inventions were performing beautifully, the Vault was better than ever.

And the Trackers were becoming a crack team of spies.

**What was Lazlo's plan? He obviously thought you needed to be ready for something big. How did he bring Shantorian out into the open?**

You remember the Glyphmaster, that puzzle Lazlo used to draw *me* out into the open? Well, Zara improved on it.

**I don't understand. What does a puzzle have to do with zip-lines and remote control cars?**

The online Glyphmaster puzzle was difficult: Strange messages had to be deciphered using a language known to only a few. It weeded people out, but more than that, it was designed as an *exclusive* game. If you didn't know the Glyph symbol language, a language I invented with a small group of other people, then you had no shot at solving the Glyphmaster puzzles.

**But you said ISD only showed the puzzle to you, no one else.**

That's true.

**I don't understand.**

Someone else solved the puzzle. Whoever it was shouldn't have even known it existed, but he did. And more importantly, he solved it ten times faster than I did.

**That's fast.**

Yeah, that's fast. Impossibly fast. Try one day for the entire thing. But the really interesting thing is the signature the solver used—the only signature Shantorian ever leaves behind, the weird-eyed kid.

*Let the record show that Adam Henderson typed three symbols into the laptop, creating Shantorian's digital signature, also known internally as* weird-eyed kid.

*O_o*

*One big eye, flat mouth, smaller eye. The fact that Mr. Henderson knows this information means one of two things: Either he's actually seen it, or he has access to RED-2 level files. This is interesting.*

**Shantorian's symbol is classified information.**

Please say you're kidding me. Anyone who spends the kind of time I do in the world of the Internet, traveling in the circles I travel in, knows about weird-eyed kid. If that's your idea of classified, your security clearance is a lot lower than I thought.

**Point taken. Continue.**

What matters here is that Shantorian found the hidden puzzle, solved it, and signed it. He did it so fast Zara was only able to collect bits and pieces of evidence, but it was enough to tell her one thing for sure: Shantorian was holed up somewhere within twenty miles of Seattle. He was close enough to catch, if only we could find him.

**Not to burst *your* bubble, but we've known Shantorian has been in the area for a while. Unfortunately there are three million people in Seattle and he's very good at hiding.**

Agreed, which is why the Glyphmaster was so important. It had drawn him out enough to narrow his location. What he needed was another reason to come out and play. So Zara developed an even harder puzzle, the GlyphMONSTER. Tougher than the first, using new symbols Zara added to the language.

She insisted on the capital letters for MONSTER whenever we typed it out in e-mails. She was proud of it.

## What was different about this new puzzle?

After reviewing Zara's code, I realized it was possible to pinpoint Shantorian's location if he tried to solve the Glyph-MONSTER. Zara had cleverly devised a digital GPS system that would do the job in under a minute, like tracing the location of a cell phone. Zara had managed to go deeper than previous online tracking systems. The code was incredible, a real work of art. She could tie a user to a physical location through a series of digital trip wires. Thirty seconds gave us a neighborhood, forty-five seconds a building. A minute on the GlyphMONSTER would give us the chair a player was sitting in.

## That's impressive. And impossible.

I'm sorry to disappoint you, but it *was* possible. I sat right there and tested it on my dad. I texted it from my phone to his laptop, said it was something I was tinkering with at camp. He didn't have a clue what he was looking at, but he tried to move some of the Glyph symbols around. The program traced him to our city block, then to the Grind House, and finally to the chair he was sitting in.

I texted him: *Enjoying that Grind House coffee?*

He answered: *Yeah, and the cookies are running seventy-three cents today. How'd you know I was here?*

Lewis and Finn were impressed, high-fiving each other on such a cool new piece of surveillance tech. But Emily was chilly. She was still having a hard time trusting Zara, and she hated it when Zara did anything that impressed the rest of us.

**Somehow I don't think a game called the GlyphMONSTER is about to catch Shantorian. Please tell me you've concocted a better story than that.**

I'm a tech wizard, not a novelist. I can't make this stuff up. No one could! But to answer your question, the game was only part of the trap. Zara knew it wouldn't be enough. We had to have something else, something bigger to lure Shantorian out into the open.

**The Raymond disk.**

You're such a good guesser. It's like you made this up, not me.

*Lieutenant Marks arrives to take Adam out for a bathroom break.*

*Raymond disk file notes: Long thought to be an urban legend, the existence of the Raymond disk has been verified in recent years. It is a single device that can access major banks and government intelligence files, disrupting financial markets and destabilizing entire regions. These two levels of power have been confirmed, but the Raymond disk has a third, even more devastating power that has not been verified. It is said the Raymond disk could permanently shut down the Internet.*

*Adam reenters the room. The interview resumes.*

**Let's assume for the moment the Raymond disk is real and by some stroke of bad luck you happened to have it. How did Zara plan to use it?**

It was Lazlo's plan, but Zara seemed to agree with it. If we could put the Raymond disk into play, Shantorian would see we'd done it and become curious.

"There's only one way Shantorian will believe we have it," Zara explained. "We'll have to activate at least one of the Raymond mechanisms."

I remember Finn saying, "Hold on, fellow crime stopper.

That Raymond dude is Trackers Kryptonite. I say we steer clear."

Lewis reminded Finn that Raymond wasn't a villain from a comic book, it was a piece of hardware loaded with complicated software.

Emily piped in next. "Actually, it's more like the ultimate Internet lockpick...with a special button that will blow everything up." She stared at Zara. "If we steal money from banks or dig around inside top secret military files, it will be evidence against us. This is a terrible idea."

But Zara had the rest of us convinced. She reminded us that Shantorian had never come out of hiding before.

"So you're saying we need a King Kong–size carrot," Finn asked. "Something so big even Shantorian can't ignore it."

"Yes, that's what she's saying," Lazlo spoke up. He had quietly crept in behind us, scaring Lewis half to death.

After a long pause, he went on: "The GlyphMONSTER should get us close, but the only way Shantorian is coming all the way out into the open is if we open up a bank. He's a criminal. I've been at this a long time, and one thing I know for certain: Money talks with criminals. All we need to do is open the door and Shantorian will walk through it. And let me make one thing clear: I'm the only adult in the room. Everything associated with this operation is on my shoulders. I found you all. I built the team. I developed the plan. If ISD fails in its mission, it will be my responsibility."

It meant a lot to me that Lazlo was willing to take the fall for the rest of us. For all his crazy tests, I was starting to respect the guy, maybe even like him. He'd given up his life to protect the world from guys like Shantorian. As far as I knew, we were the only family he had, and he was putting everything on the line, trusting us not to fail.

**Before we go on, tell me once more the state of the Raymond disk at this time.**

When I got Raymond from Lazlo, it was a microchip, not a complete disk, about half the size of a postage stamp and not much thicker. I guess you could say I was the one who changed it from the Raymond chip to the Raymond disk, because now it's got a housing I made out of an old flash drive casing. It's still small, about the size of a ChapStick. I'd know it instantly if I saw it. Either way, chip or disk, the more time I spent with the Raymond device, the more clearly I saw what it really was: a parasite. Raymond changes when it's connected to a computer; it needs a host in order to do its job. And there's a lot of programming involved, millions of lines of code.

**Can you produce the Raymond disk?**

You mean, do I have it on me? Can't say that I do.

**So you're saying you lost one of the most precious technological assets in the history of the world. Nice job, superspy.**

I have a feeling it's going to turn up at some point, but right now I have no idea where it is.

**Moving on, then — it sounds like Zara and Emily didn't get along too well.**

You got that right. It was bad enough at the start, but a few days later, it got even worse.

**Why?**

We'd failed another surveillance test, which was becoming a bad habit. The test would have gone fine if we'd had a different kind of equipment. What we really needed was a small camera that could drive, like a car. It had to be small, it had to have superzoom, and, ideally, it would drive up walls.

I know, tall order. But it was apparent from the test that this was exactly the kind of device Lazlo wished we had.

"I can build one," I remember Emily saying. "Let me and Lewis have a camera and access to the right tools. I bet we can develop something that will work."

Finn and I both shrugged, but he had to be thinking the same thing I was: *Good luck with that.*

The next day, to everyone's surprise, Emily and Lewis had something to show us. They gathered everyone in the hangar, including Lazlo, and unveiled what Emily called the TruckCam.

"Fire it up, Lewis!" Emily said. She was holding a modified Belinski controller, staring down at one of her RC monster trucks. It roared to life, spewing tiny flames out the tailpipe.

"You can watch right here," Lewis told us, pointing to his laptop as the screen lit up. Emily swiveled the camera view and the screen responded. The TruckCam was loud and way too big, but at least the camera was doing its job, which was something. And really, this was a first gen prototype, so if it worked at all, it could be our first step in the right direction.

"Check this out," Emily said.

The TruckCam lurched forward with a strange popping sound, and I realized along with everyone else that Emily and Lewis had modified the tires. They were covered in small orange suction cups, which grabbed at the floor as it moved. It sounded like someone was jumping up and down on a sheet of Bubble Wrap.

When the TruckCam neared the wall of the hangar, Lewis yelled, "Gun it!"

Emily hit the gas hard, lifting the front wheels of the TruckCam into the air.

"Brakes!" Lewis screamed.

Emily slammed on the brakes. The TruckCam's front wheels hit the wall and everything went quiet. The TruckCam had stalled.

"Hang on, I got this," said Finn, trying to be supportive in what was becoming a disastrous embarrassment. He hopped on his board, rode to the wall, and flipped the restart switch.

"All systems go!" he yelled.

A few seconds later, the TruckCam was ten feet off the ground, popping and revving its way up the wall on four suction-cupped tires. It turned a wide circle, pointing toward the floor, and Emily proclaimed the camera to be in position.

The TruckCam engine died another death.

## What did you do then?

We all stared at the laptop screen, because no one wanted to catch Emily's eye.

"You want me to start it up again?" yelled Finn. "I could grab a ladder."

But Finn wasn't going to need a ladder to get the Truck-Cam down, because three seconds later, the suction cups failed. Finn tried to catch the falling equipment, but Finn being Finn, we could hardly expect him to save a falling object.

Metal, glass, and orange suction cups flew everywhere when the TruckCam slammed into the concrete floor, but I kept looking at the blank laptop screen.

"This is only a prototype," Lewis said. "We're still testing it."

Lazlo didn't say a word. He just stared, as if he wasn't so much disappointed as amazed at what he'd just seen.

Then Zara stepped forward and things got really ugly.

**Let me guess: Zara had some ideas of her own about what to build?**

Way worse. Not only did Zara have some ideas, she'd used those ideas to build the Orville DC, which was everything the TruckCam was not.

**Tell me more.**

While Emily and Lewis's invention smoldered in a heap of ruins, Zara pulled a small white box out of her pocket and set it on the floor. It was the size of two decks of cards, one stacked on top of the other.

"Interesting," Lazlo said. He moved in for a closer look. We all did.

"What is it?" Finn asked.

"I took the liberty of asking Lazlo for some specifications," Zara said.

"Specifications for what, a mouse house?" Finn couldn't help himself—and to be fair, whatever Zara had built didn't look like much. I fully expected it to flop even more spectacularly than the TruckCam had.

Zara explained: "Lazlo gave us two tests in a row where we were expected to place a camera high on a wall without being seen. I just figured there was a reason, so I asked Lazlo what he was looking for. He said small, white, superzoom. So I took what he told me and created something. I call it the Orville DC."

I asked what the DC stood for and Zara continued explaining.

"I hope you don't mind—I had to alter the Deckard code for a smaller lens."

I didn't have to look at Lewis to know his heart had just sunk. Zara was putting superzoom into play, an area in which Lewis was supposed to be an expert. Not only that, she'd suggested right out of the gate that she could do it smaller, which in technology terms usually means *better*. I felt my own competitive nature kick in at the thought of Zara creating a gadget that rivaled one of my own.

"May I?" Zara asked, taking a step closer to the only computer in the hangar. Lewis looked like he didn't know what to do—hang on to the laptop, hand it over, or run away. Zara reached out slowly, like she had encountered a stray dog, and started typing on the keyboard.

A few seconds later, the screen changed. We were seeing what the Orville DC saw as it took off across the floor. The Orville DC was virtually silent until it reached the wall. Then, like magic, it effortlessly climbed straight up, turned on a dime, and parked. There was a slight sound as it climbed the wall, but when it parked, the hangar was deathly quiet again.

"How'd you do that?" I asked her.

"Vacuum technology gets it up there. After that, it's microglue. The Orville DC is light, so there's not much to hold. When I hit park, it uses an extra vacuum burst to retract the wheels and inject a stream of microglue. On a flat surface it adheres instantly."

"How do we get it back?" Emily asked.

Zara clicked a button on the remote and the sound returned. We all watched as the Orville DC zigzagged wildly on the wall and reparked.

"The wheels reengage with the wall and we're back to the vacuum," she explained. "It's pretty basic."

If I remember right, which I always do, Finn's response went like this:

"Microglue and vacuum technology? Let me at that thing!"

Zara handed over the controls and I quickly took them before Finn could run the Orville DC into the floor and kill it. Zara hadn't had enough experience with Finn to realize how dangerous it was to put expensive equipment in his hands.

The remote was small so it could be easily hidden from view in a crowded place. I handed it to Lewis, who graciously took it. He zoomed in on Lazlo's face, expertly managing the Deckard controls as we all stared at the laptop. What Lazlo said surprised all of us.

"I think we're ready to visit a bank."

**I bet that drove some spikes between Zara and the Trackers.**

Not as much as you might think. We all loved gadgets and we were dying to get out of training mode and into a real-world situation. Zara had taken my work, added to it, and created something amazing. The Orville DC was exactly what Lazlo had hoped for. Emily couldn't deny it; none of us could. No doubt I was envious of Zara's achievement, but we were going into the field and we had Zara to thank for that. It would have been nice if she'd have included me, but honestly, I wished even more that I had come up with the new device on my own. Given the same opportunity myself, I'd have done the same thing. I'd have holed up in the Vault, shut everyone out, and emerged with a new device of my own.

If any of us had asked Lazlo, he'd have told us, but we didn't. I actually think Emily respected Zara more after that.

## What about Lewis? This must have hit him pretty hard.

Yeah, he got a little homesick after that. It had to feel like someone was invading his area of expertise. But he bounced back. Lewis isn't the kind of guy to carry a grudge; he's too nice for that. Now Emily, *she* can carry a grudge.

That night I worked really late. I had a major breakthrough just after midnight and went looking for Lewis. I knew he'd be excited for me. Finn was totally zonked out, but I found Lewis sitting at one of the Xbox stations playing a racing game.

"You don't even like racing games," I said, sitting down next to him.

"Yeah, I know," he replied.

"So why are you playing one?" I asked.

Lewis crashed the car he was driving into a wall and stared at the floor.

"I'm thinking I might go home," he confessed.

I knew Lewis well enough to realize he was just down and needed someone to pick him up. He wasn't a quitter, not by a long shot.

"You can't go home," I told him. "I won't let you."

This didn't work. "What's the point of my being here anyway?" Lewis asked. "Everything is going mobile—the Orville helicopter cam, and now this...this Deckard Orville whatever she calls it."

"The Orville DC."

"Whatever. The point is, I'm no good with remote controls. Everything seems backward to me."

"You're still the best zoomer we've got," I assured him. "Remember what you did with that church steeple? If it wasn't for you, we wouldn't even be *in* ISD. We'd be hanging out at the Grind House. Dude, you got us in, and your moment will come. I promise."

It took quite a bit of convincing to get Lewis to stay, so I didn't have the heart to tell him about my programming breakthrough.

When I returned to the Vault, Lazlo was waiting for me. He was like that, always appearing out of nowhere when you least expected him.

"Are you ready?" he asked me.

I knew what he was talking about without him having to explain. The primary thing I'd been working on since our arrival at the hangar was the Raymond disk. I'd activated it before, but it was more complicated to open the banks in a way that would both cover our tracks and allow us to keep them open for an extended period of time. Running the Raymond disk was actually a lot more complicated than I'd originally thought, so I'm skipping a bunch of details here that I'll get back to later. For now, all you need to know is that I had to write new code for running the program over a series of hundreds of wireless routers in different cities across the globe. It was a weeklong brain-melter, but I'd done it.

**I have a feeling we've arrived at Lazlo's plan.**

I don't suppose I could hope for some nachos and a Coke?

**Keep talking. I'll order us a cheese pizza.**

A pizza. You're not going soft on me, are you?

**Even agents get hungry at this hour. Just keep talking.**

The next morning Lazlo summoned all of us to his personal office, which was clear on the other side of the hangar, all by itself. He was a private guy. There was our little corner of the world and there was his, and in between a hundred yards of concrete. All of us but Finn piled into one of the old golf carts and we pulled Finn back and forth across the hangar while he laughed and did tricks. Finn was good for blowing off steam when we were nervous, and *boy* were we nervous. This was it. This was the debriefing before we'd activate the Raymond disk at a real bank.

**And you had no reservations about what you were getting yourself into? It didn't cross your mind that you were about to open up the vaults of the biggest banks in the world?**

Yeah, but we weren't going to take anything. We *didn't* take anything. I've been telling you that all night, but you won't listen.

**All evidence is to the contrary. But I'd love to hear what you're going to lie about next.**

I wish you'd stop calling me a liar.

**I wish you'd start telling the truth.**

Lady, that's all I've done for ten hours and counting. I can't make you believe me. All I've got is my freaky accurate memory and a pile of evidence, which clearly isn't enough for you. But you know what? The truth is all I'm going to need to save my friends and set the record straight. Just wait, you'll see.

**You mean this story gets even better? I can hardly wait. Tell me—what happened when you arrived at Lazlo's private office?**

He was on the phone, so we waited outside and watched Finn do thirty kick flips in a row. When Lazlo finally came out, he didn't say a word, just ushered us into his office and sat us down. I remember that meeting, every detail.

Lazlo spoke: "Before we begin, Zara has something to tell us, don't you, Zara?"

She dropped a bombshell. "Shantorian is on the move. He took the bait."

"That was fast," I remember saying. And it was. He'd already figured out the first level, which was no small accomplishment. I'd been on there for hours and gotten nowhere.

"The most amazing thing about the solve is how little

time he was actually on the site," Zara went on. "By my records, he was only there for seven seconds, which means he somehow managed to pull all the code off the server and solve off-line."

I told her that was impossible, and based on my review of the setup, it was. The program simply would not run off-line.

"There's no other way he could have done it," Zara told me. "He back-doored the system. He hacked us."

I'd spent hours looking at the GlyphMONSTER from every angle imaginable, and I hadn't found a way to access the underlying code. This guy was incredible.

**Pizza's on the way. Gotta love the Internet.**

Are you even listening to me?

**Shantorian solved the first level. Got it.**

*Agent notation: He's getting tired. I can see it in his eyes. He's going to make a mistake.*

Maybe this will get your attention: Lazlo had been staking out a bank for months, building a relationship with a systemwide vice president of operations. This guy managed, like, a hundred branches, which gave him the kind of access we needed. Lazlo had been to this guy's office a dozen times, which was in this super-high-end bank.

According to Lazlo, he'd earned this VP's trust. He was a sitting duck.

Lazlo and Emily were going in at three o'clock sharp, and the new Orville DC was going to get its first real-world test.

**So Zara made the technology, but Lazlo chose Emily to use it? That doesn't make a lot of sense.**

It does if you're a master of surveillance.

Lazlo laid the entire thing out for us, telling us Zara would stay in the hangar, monitoring the GlyphMONSTER. We needed to be alert if Shantorian showed himself again. Emily would enter the bank with Lazlo, posing as his niece.

"This banker has a habit of leaving his door ajar when we meet in the common space of the bank to discuss business," Lazlo informed us. "When he comes out to greet us, Emily will create a diversion and we'll put the Orville DC into play."

The rest of us would wait in a surveillance van outside. It would be my job to man the controls of the Orville DC, getting it into the private office and up on the wall where it couldn't be seen. And it had to be perfect. If the camera couldn't zoom in on the computer screen at the right angle, we'd never see it.

**See what?**

The unlock code. Every bank in the world uses the same security code once every seven days. If the code isn't entered, money can't flow freely between that bank and all the others. It's something the Raymond disk didn't account for, because that level of security wasn't around when the program was made.

Sure, the Raymond codes could open a back door to bank accounts, and money could be taken out. The problem? There's no way to hide what you're doing. All the accounts are connected, one way or another, and eventually the money would be found. But the security codes gave us a different level of entry. Raymond got us in, but the codes would do something more: allow us to roam around inside the digital world of the banks without being seen.

**So having the security code made you, what, invisible?**

That's right. We had a feeling Shantorian knew about this, but didn't have the nerve to actually enter a bank. He was a recluse, I figured, and there was only one way to get this code: inside a bank.

Would you like to see what happened?

**Actually, your timing couldn't be better. Our pizza has arrived.**

*Food and drinks were placed in the room, Adam did his usual magic at the keyboard, and I watched as the security of the world's banks was compromised.*

*Note: A transcript of this video appears in Appendix M, page 138.*

www.trackersinterface.com

PASSWORD

AGENTSMITH

**That's some fairly incredible footage.**

Starting to believe me now?

**It depends on what you mean by *believe*. I can't help but think these things happened. How else would you have a video like that? Impossible to stage. But make no mistake — billions of dollars are still missing. Nothing you've shown me so far leads me to believe you didn't take it.**

Then I guess I better keep going.

**I guess you better.**

Lazlo knew the security code was changed once every seven days. The code came in on a Monday, got entered at the start and end of every business day, and at the end of the week it was replaced with a fresh code. The Orville DC got the footage we needed of the banker typing in the security code, and I'd done my job on the Raymond disk. You'll notice from the footage that we also tapped into the bank surveillance cameras. That was a bit of my own handiwork, not as hard as it looks since all the feeds were wireless.

**So wireless is easier to tap into?**

49

Night and day. People think their wireless data is safe, but that kind of security cracks like an egg.

**Tell me what Lazlo planned to do next.**

As of ten o'clock that night, we had set the entire trap. If I hit the right button, the Raymond disk would activate and open all the digital vaults we could get our hands on. We could look in, but no one would know we were there. Entering the security code from our remote location gave us the ability to gather up money from different accounts without being seen.

"Dude, you really gonna push that button?" I remember Finn asking me.

I'd told everyone to come into the Vault so I could show off my work. Shantorian might have been able to solve the GlyphMONSTER in scary fast time, but me? I'd unlocked every bank on the planet. I'd taken an ancient technology and hot-wired it, creating the most dangerous hack the world had ever seen.

**Did you activate the bank protocol? Answer carefully, Adam. This one really matters.**

I did. Emily, Finn, and Lewis? They just stood there. It was one hundred percent me opening up those banks so Shantorian could see inside. But I believed I was doing it for the right reasons. I still do.

**And yet there is this pesky problem of the missing billions. You know where the money is. Why not simply tell me?**

Because you won't understand how it got where it is unless you hear the whole story.

That night I spent hours on the GlyphMONSTER, hoping to figure out Zara's logic, but there was another reason why I stayed on it, and Emily made sure I knew what it was.

"You want to impress her, don't you?" she asked me. It was after midnight and I was cranky.

"No," I told her, "I just want to figure it out."

"Maybe if you spent a little more time thinking about your friends you'd realize we're in trouble," she said.

I asked her what she meant.

"I mean the Trackers," she told me. "*Us.* The way it used to be. We're not a team anymore."

"Sure we are," I said. "We'll always be a team."

"Tell that to Lewis," she replied. End of conversation.

When she went into the girls' dorm room, I headed for the hangar. I knew Lewis would be out there practicing, and sure enough, I saw him, way out in the middle, all by himself. Zara had rigged up a second remote control Orville DC, only this one had no camera. It was strictly for practicing on the controls. I drove the golf cart out there and parked next to him, watching as he struggled to navigate a test course of cones he'd set up. I was particularly nervous about him, because it would be his job to retrieve the Orville DC from the bank.

**Hold on a minute. Lazlo chose Lewis to retrieve the camera? Why?**

It was likely to take most of the day—getting over there, staking it out, doing the job, and driving back to the hangar. Zara and I needed to stay on Shantorian, and I needed more time with the Raymond disk. Emily and Lazlo would go back in for the retrieval. Plus, there was the thing no one wanted to talk about: We could get caught. If that happened, our two best programmers would need to shut everything down and cover our tracks.

**So it was imperative that Lewis master the controls?**

It was. When I approached Lewis that night, it was clear he was making progress. Lazlo would be pleased.

"Hey, you're getting better with that thing," I told him.

His answer was typical modest Lewis: "Funny, it feels like I'm getting worse. The controls are really touchy, especially the wall climbing."

"You'll do fine," I assured him. "How are you feeling about tomorrow?"

Lewis shrugged, but didn't look up from the work he was doing. We both heard Finn coming toward us on his skateboard, no doubt looking for someone to pull him around behind a golf cart. He couldn't stay up and do any work after midnight, but he was good to go if anyone wanted to play.

"Man, I'm hungry," he said as he pulled up beside us.

"What I wouldn't give for a cheeseburger and fries! The food here is killing me."

He was right, the food was pretty bad. How many peanut butter and jelly sandwiches and bowls of ramen noodles could they expect us to eat?

Finn changed subjects. "I was checking out the GlyphMONSTER in the vault," he said. "Those new icons are way better than anything you ever came up with."

"Thanks a lot," I replied.

He had a point. Zara had used a monster motif for the upgraded version of her puzzle. There were only ten symbols, but every one of them was awesome:

Godzilla, King Kong, Rodan, Mothra, Wolfman, Zombie, Frankenstein, Jaws, Dracula, and T. rex.

The icons were retro-cool, but that didn't make the puzzle any easier to solve. I'd tried mixing the letters from the names, putting them in date or release order, and a hundred other scenarios. For the life of me I could not find a hidden message in the GlyphMONSTER.

We talked a little more, and then I convinced Lewis to go back with us and get some sleep. We were all wiped out.

Two days passed without word from Shantorian, and we started to think maybe we'd lost him. The worst part of those two days? I started to believe Emily was right. The Trackers just weren't the same as we once were.

Finn didn't have enough to do. He was best when he was out on a mission, but we were locked down doing surveillance. "TechBaseTen is boring" was something he said a lot. Also,

"What's it gonna take to get some better video games?" and "Are you sure Domino's won't deliver out here? They *gotta* deliver out here!"

Emily and Zara were hanging out more, a result of the girls' dorm, no doubt. It was just the two of them, and while there was some serious competition, they also seemed to lean on each other for moral support.

And then there was Lewis. He just plain disappeared. He'd spend tons of time in the guys' dorm working on his laptop. Other times he'd go out and ride laps around the hangar on his bike. We lost track of him for hours at a time, and there was one stretch where I couldn't find him for the better part of an entire morning.

And then, like a little miracle, something happened. Something big.

Shantorian contacted us.

**Okay, you have my full attention now.**

It was more than just working on the puzzle. He sent us a video message.

**So you saw him? That's a video I'd very much like to see.**

I know, right? Because no one has ever seen what he looks like. Don't get your hopes up. We didn't *see* him. But we sure got a better idea of who he was.

Scary guy. Scary ideas.

And there was something weird about how we got the message, too.

He delivered it through Lewis.

**I don't understand.**

Lewis always checked the mail, because the mailbox was way the heck down this long road. Lazlo wouldn't let us take the golf cart all the way down there, but Lewis had a bike, so the job fell to him. Sometimes I'd watch him ride out there and back on one of the outside cameras hooked to the Vault. It was kind of sad, really, because I could tell he was down. He'd do these wide turns back and forth, like he wasn't in any rush to return to the hangar.

That's how I knew something had happened, because when I watched him that day, he was riding back straight as an arrow, as fast as his bike would carry him.

## Shantorian used snail mail?

Yup, very old-school. At first, when Lewis said he'd gotten a package, Finn couldn't help himself.

"I hope it's fresh socks from your mom, 'cause the ones you've been wearing are starting to make my eyes water," he said. "If it's from your parents, they probably sent candy, too. Don't hold out on us, bro!"

Lewis dropped the bomb.

"It's not from my parents. It's from Shantorian."

We were all like, no way, that can't be. But Lewis handed over a flash drive, which he'd taken out of a single manila envelope. There was no return address, which could only mean one thing: The message had arrived without passing through the postal service. These days you can't even send a simple letter without a return address.

## I know how the U.S. Postal Service works. It's my job to know. Go on.

Shantorian had scratched his weird-eyed kid signature on the side of the flash drive. O_o. It was the only marking that gave away who it might be from.

Zara was quick to remind us: "We need to be careful with that thing. I don't think we should open it on the network."

She was right, of course. Knowing Shantorian, the disk was capable of unleashing a virus on every computer in the hangar. Lewis's laptop wasn't tied into the network, so we used his.

Are you ready to hear what the legend had to say?

**Just show me the evidence.**

*Agent notation: It is nearing 4:00 A.M. Mr. Henderson has loaded an important piece of new evidence and told me the password. The kid's got stamina, I'll give him that. I have a feeling the sun's going to come up before we come to the end.*

*Note: A transcript of this video appears in Appendix N, page 143.*

**So this is why you wanted to see Lewis earlier, because you don't trust him. He turned on you once, so he might do it again.**

There was no doubt at that moment: We all realized something had fundamentally changed. We didn't trust each other anymore, and it wasn't just Lewis. The conversation we had after watching that video told me everything I needed to know about how far we'd come from where we used to be.

"That you, Lewis?" was the first salvo, thrown by Finn. I could tell it hurt to even ask. "Say it ain't so."

Lewis just shook his head unconvincingly.

"Lewis, just tell us the truth," I said. "Who is that guy and what were you giving him?"

"Leave him alone!" Emily yelled. She actually stood between me and Lewis, like she was protecting him from flying fists. "He said it's not him, so it's not him."

"Tell me this, then," said Zara. "Where does he go all day long? We're in here, working, but he seems to vanish."

"You don't even know us," Emily shot back. "And I could say the same thing about you. All day long you sit in that room, but no one's allowed in. You say you're working on code, but how do we know what you're *really* doing?"

"I can defend myself," Lewis said.

I remember thinking I wanted to trust him, that it meant everything. Because you know what? The foundation of the

Trackers wasn't the gadgets or the missions or ISD, it was trust. If we'd lost that, it was over. We might as well all go home.

"That's not me," Lewis said. "And if you must know what I've been doing all day long, I was learning how to run a remote control camera so I can get back in charge of the Deckard."

Lewis pulled out the controller for the Orville DC, set the test car on the floor, and proceeded to put it through its paces right there in the hangar. He ran it under tables, through Finn's legs, into the guys' dorm where he couldn't even see it, then parked it right in front of Lazlo. Lazlo picked it up, spun its wheels.

"ISD is built on trust," he said. "It's one of the reasons I chose all of you. What we're doing is dangerous, possibly life threatening. We're going after a criminal mastermind. He's smarter than each of us, but not smarter than *all* of us. My guess? Shantorian made it himself to toy with us."

"It would make sense," Finn said. I could tell he wanted to believe Lazlo, would talk himself into it if he could. "He'd try to weaken us so he could have the upper hand. This guy is smooth."

**But you didn't believe Lewis, did you?**

No, I didn't. I wanted to as badly as Finn and Emily did. But it went deeper than that. Looking at all the faces in that room, I realized I didn't trust anyone anymore. Not one of them. Someone, possibly more than one member of ISD, wasn't telling the truth. Something wasn't right.

"There's one way to find out if he's all the way in." This was Zara's answer to the problem, and it was risky. "Let Lewis run the remote at the bank today. Let him get the Deckard back."

"No problem," Emily said, raring to get Lewis on the controls and prove he was still an important part of the team.

"I'll go with you guys," Finn said. "Let these two programmers do their thing in peace."

It felt oddly as if Zara and I were aligned together in one corner, with the rest of the Trackers together in another, and Lazlo standing back to watch what would happen. Maybe he imagined this as a test of our mettle, but more likely, we all saw it as a necessary course of events.

**How do you mean?**

There was something else on the flash drive Shantorian sent us.

**Another video?**

No, instructions.

**What kind of instructions?**

The kind that can turn the world upside down.

**You mean the red button?**

Yup, I mean the red button. Of all the things we had learned about since Lazlo came into our lives, the red button was the most incredible. The power to shut down the Internet, to render it useless, even for an hour, was such a big idea I always had trouble wrapping my brain around it. These days, the Internet really is a web, one the entire planet is caught in. It was as if the spider were about to eat its prey.

**Interesting analogy, but why shut down the Internet? What would be the point? The banks were already open.**

Shantorian knew something we didn't. The only way money could be moved without a trace was if the whole system was blinded. There had to be a blackout, a moment when everyone was asleep but one person. And Shantorian wanted that one person to be me.

**Quite an honor.**

More like a burden. The programming Shantorian sent over would need to be integrated and tested. He would need to see that I'd figured it out before he'd come all the way out into the open and trust us. What he was proposing was an alteration to the red button, one that would shut the system down for every-one but us. The grid might be asleep, but I could move things around at will, or at least my workstation could.

**Sounds complicated.**

And time-consuming. It looked like a million hours of work. But this is what he wanted, this window inside, and I was the guy to make it happen. While I was doing Shantorian's work, Zara needed to use all her skills to track his location. There had to be clues in his movements, if only she could decipher them. The second we found him, the FBI would be informed and—bang!—we'd catch the world's greatest hacker. The thought of it sent chills, let me tell you.

**So even though you didn't trust him, Lewis was back in?**

He had to be. It was clear he'd learned how to run the con-trols. Emily couldn't do it because we needed her inside the bank. Zara and I had a mountain of programming to do and we were quickly running out of time. Finn was more likely to crash the Orville DC than get it out of there safely—he's a better wingman than a pilot.

And, hey, if Lewis could do this job without intention-ally framing the rest of the team or otherwise sabotaging the mission, I was ready to trust him again. But it was risky, no doubt. It showed me once again how deep in Lazlo was. He was willing to take incredible risks in order to catch

Shantorian. I mean, like he'd said, he was the only adult in the room.

This was all on him.

**Sounds like you were really starting to respect what Lazlo was doing.**

Sure I was. We all were. Like I've been saying, the guy basically gave up everything to save the world.

**So Lazlo, Emily, Finn, and Lewis left for the bank?**

Lazlo scheduled a meeting with the bank manager for one thirty, after the lunch rush so the bank would be a little on the quiet side. Zara went to her private coding room and I worked in the Vault, but after about a half hour I knocked on her door. Emily's comment had rattled me—why was Zara so private? She yelled for me to come in but didn't look up from her work. I never saw anyone so focused, which made me see how she could learn about anything she set her mind to.

She asked me how progress was going on the new code.

"I've only been at it a little while," I said, "but I can tell you this much: It's going to be a late night."

"Ditto," she told me. "There are moments when I feel so close to catching this guy. It's like he's six steps ahead of me on a chessboard. I see a pattern, follow it until I think it's going to reveal something, and then it disappears, and a new pattern appears. The guy is amazing."

"Could be he's just trying to keep you busy," I suggested. "Our best programmer lost down a bunch of rabbit holes. That's what I'd do."

I figured she'd be angry with me, telling her she was probably being duped and all, but she turned and looked my way, her beauty not the least bit diminished by lack of sleep.

"You think I'm the best programmer?" she asked me.

"Sure, you're the best," I answered. "Who'd you think it was, Finn? News flash, that guy couldn't program his way out of a paper bag."

But I knew what she meant. If she was the best, then I was second best.

"Let's just say he's got us both running around like squirrels for the moment," Zara said. "Let's show him who he's dealing with."

In its own way, this was like a little pep talk, and I was glad I'd gone in to see her. I was excited to get cracking, but I wasn't ready to let her go just yet.

"I trust you. You know that, right?" I asked her.

"I trust you, too, Adam. Now let's catch this Shantorian guy and put him behind bars where he belongs."

"Sounds like a plan," I said.

**One big, happy family. How sweet.**

Yeah, well, we tried at least.

**What happened at the bank?**

Zara and I stayed focused for, I don't know, maybe three hours. Then Emily called me on the Trinity, her face appearing on one of the Vault cameras. Lazlo was driving, but Finn was right next to her.

"We got it back, no problem," Finn reported. "Lewis was awesome. The guy was a total champ on the controls."

"There's just one problem," Emily continued.

"It's not a problem unless we make it one." This was Lazlo from the driver's seat.

"Where's Lewis?" I asked.

"That's the problem," Emily said. "He's gone."

Emily held up the Orville DC controller, which had been left behind on the seat. When Lazlo and Emily returned from inside the bank, they found Finn eating an apple, but no Lewis.

"I tried to stop him," Finn said. "I even chased alongside on my board, but the guy is fast on that bike. I lost him."

It turns out Lewis had packed his bike in the back of the surveillance van while no one was paying attention. Finn had tried to reason with him, but Lewis wouldn't budge.

"He said he didn't want any part of the Trackers anymore," Finn told us, shaking his head. "That hurt, but the guy's got a point. I mean, we turned on him a little bit, you know?"

Emily just glared into the screen, didn't say a word. Lewis had spent countless hours learning how to control the Orville DC. He'd performed admirably, and my thanks was to distrust him over a video anyone could have made. The Trackers were falling apart and it was my fault. And you want to know the worst part? I still didn't trust Lewis. I mean, why run off like that? Maybe he *was* working with Shantorian, and that's why Shantorian knew so much. Or—and this was an insane thought—maybe Lewis *was* Shantorian. Okay, fantasy over, but *something* was up. I couldn't for the life of me figure out what it was, which probably had something to do with getting zero sleep.

**You seem to be doing just fine on zero sleep right now. You were suspicious—that makes sense. Where did Lewis go?**

No one knew. He just disappeared. But I was so consumed by the work I had to do I didn't have time to worry about mending what was broken. I had to keep slinging code. We'd have to find Lewis once the job was done.

**So you kept on programming?**

Yup. Everyone else but me and Zara crashed around midnight. Somewhere around two in the morning, I fell asleep in the Vault with my hand on the mouse. It would take something big to put a bounce back in my step, and that's exactly what I got at around three.

"Adam, get in here," were the words I heard. The voice became part of my dream, in which I was chasing Shantorian on Finn's skateboard, crashing into a garbage dumpster in a dark alley.

"Adam, wake up!"

I jumped awake, and there was Zara's face staring down at me from a monitor in the Vault. How was it she could look so put together in the middle of the night? I could already imagine what I must look like, hair standing on end, dribble coming out the corner of my mouth.

"Get in here!" she yelled again, and I was up and moving across the open space between the Vault and her programming room.

"Sorry, just dozed off for a second there, what's up?" I said as I entered Zara's domain. To my surprise, Lazlo was standing next to her.

"I've been checking on you for the past hour and you've been sound asleep," Zara said, outing me in front of Lazlo.

"No matter," said Lazlo. He looked at me with just the slightest disappointment and I withered, mad at myself.

Zara pointed to her screen and said, "Shantorian has unlocked the last level of the GlyphMONSTER and accessed the video."

"No way" was the only way I could think to reply.

## What video?

If Shantorian unlocked the last level of the puzzle, he'd need a message from us, some sort of congratulations, like Zara had done to me with the Glyphmaster. It had to be something that would give him an ultimatum.

We watched Zara's video, which I'd seen before, as she spoke directly to Shantorian. She told him we were ready to push the red button (which we were not, since I'd fallen asleep on the job). She also told him we had to meet in person at the hangar. If the two parties were going to drain bank accounts of billions, they'd have to work together, each taking their turn. It would take planning, all in one room together, to pull off the heist of the century.

**What was his answer?**

I could show you, if you'd like.

**So he sent a video of his own?**

He did. Let's just say things were about to get totally crazy.

**Show me.**

*Note: A transcript of this video appears in Appendix O, page 146.*

**You know what, Adam?**

What?

**I'm actually starting to believe you, a little bit.**

But you still think I stole the money?

**No doubt in my mind.**

Even after everything I've said and everything I've shown you?

*Especially* **after everything you've said and shown me. You and I both know where this is leading. Why not cut to the chase and tell me where it is?**

Sorry to disappoint you, but you'll have to stay up a little longer.

**Have it your way, but the sun will be up soon and I know you have a way of nodding off in the middle of the night.**

Very funny.

**So the facts of the latest communication from Shantorian, if I've got this right, are these:**

- **He agreed to meet with you at the hangar.**
- **He provided a list of banks that were his, another list that was yours.**
- **He said the entire operation, if you set things up correctly, would take less than five minutes.**
- **After that, the Internet would be started back up again, the heist totally untraceable.**

You left out the part about us picking him up.

### Does that strike you as particularly important?

Well, there were only three reasons I could think of for why he would put us in control like that: blind, too old to drive, or too young to drive. The blind option seemed beyond unlikely. Super old, like too old and frail to drive? That also struck me as hard to imagine. That left too young to have a license. Something about the thought of a kid messing with us from the basement of his parents' house really bothered me. It couldn't be a kid, not with everything Shantorian could do. Impossible, right? I tried to think of other reasons why our archnemesis would want us to pick him up, but nothing else made sense.

### And there was still no sign of Lewis?

No sign at all. He'd vanished. And I know what you're thinking: Lewis is looking more and more like a mole, someone who was not what he seemed from the very beginning. I'll admit there's some merit to the idea. The quiet, nervous one in the bunch. The guy you'd least expect. How long had I really known Lewis? A couple of years. Maybe he wasn't what he seemed. Maybe he was even older than he appeared and just posing as a fifteen-year-old.

**Could be he's a middle-aged Hungarian with lots of plastic surgery.**

You're making fun of me.

**A little bit.**

So you don't think Lewis is Shantorian?

**I didn't say that. We're getting off the point. Several billion dollars is missing. You're stalling and I'm running very low on patience.**

Give me another hour, two at the most, and I promise, I'll show you the money.

**Take me through the rest of that evening, once you knew you were going to see Shantorian and you weren't ready with the programming.**

I can give you the short version in one word: *chaos.* It was the middle of the night but sleep was out of the question. Shantorian was going to be standing in the hangar. The very thought of it sent Finn into a fit of excitement.

"If we get him into the hangar he's got no shot," he told us. "We'll own his code-slinging butt!"

Even Emily and Zara were high-fiving each other, something I didn't think I'd ever see. The idea of catching Shantorian was pulsing through the hangar like an electric charge.

It took Lazlo to set us back a notch, the same steady calm in his voice we'd all come to appreciate.

"I understand your enthusiasm," he said, "but let me remind you who we're dealing with. Shantorian has never been seen, and certainly never been caught. We've set an elaborate, well-crafted trap and he appears to have taken the bait. But there's one thing we can be sure of: He's got something up his sleeve."

"We know this, Lazlo," Finn piped in. "No way we're letting you down when it really matters."

Lazlo had been chasing Shantorian for a decade, maybe longer, and the whole operation was coming to a head. We all nodded, agreeing with what Finn had said. Letting Lazlo down wasn't an option.

The next twelve hours were a total blur. I've never been that energized in my entire life. It was like an adrenaline rush that kept going and going. My mind was sharper than it's ever been. No Red Bull, no Mountain Dew, just total focus on the task at hand.

Emily and Finn wired up dozens of new cameras, blasting through the hangar on the golf cart and climbing endlessly through the web of catwalks. They placed cameras all throughout the main landing area, where the Vault sat, because we were pretty sure Shantorian would enter through the front door. Outside, zoom cameras were added so we could see anyone approaching from a distance and follow them all the way up the drive. Every time a new camera was in place, Emily called it into the Vault and I created a wireless recording feed. If Shantorian showed his face, we would get it on tape.

Zara worked tirelessly on scripts that would trigger backup traces from each of the bank systems Shantorian had given us. This was vitally important, because even if we caught him in the act, we had to make sure we could trace the money if he actually shut down the Internet. If he opened the banks, took the money, accessed intelligence files, and shut down the Internet for even a split second, we would capture it all. The money might move, but Zara's scripts would protect the assets from disappearing.

**And yet you say you have no idea where the money went.**

I never said that.

**So you do know where it is?**

Well, sure I do. I'm just not ready to tell you yet.

**You're making a big mistake. The longer you hold out on me the more trouble you and your friends are in. Just tell me where it is. Now.**

I'm parched. Could I get some water?

**No.**

You're mean.

**And you're a criminal.**

Am not.

**Prove it. Show me the money.**

You're not the only one who can play hardball, you know. How about if we just terminate this interview right now? What if I just stop talking?

*A pitcher of water was brought in for Henderson.*

**Please, continue.**

By seven o'clock all the surveillance equipment was in place and we were down to the last details of programming. All the code from Shantorian was in place with the Raymond disk: banks, intel, and the red button were active. All they needed was a little push from Shantorian and we'd have all the evidence we'd need to put him away for a long, long time.

Zara took a short break at seven thirty to gather with us and hear one last time from Lazlo before he left.

"You've surpassed even my high expectations," he praised. And this was a big deal, because praise was not something Lazlo offered very often. When he said you'd done well, then you really knew you'd achieved something great.

I told everyone I wished Lewis hadn't left, and we all agreed it just wasn't the same without him. We were still the Trackers, but man, it sure felt hollow having the heart of your team ripped out.

"He'll come around," Finn said, ever the optimist. "Once

we get done with this mission, we'll pull him back in. You'll see."

I wasn't so sure, and I could tell by the look on Lazlo's face that he wasn't, either. I think we both worried about Lewis more than the others. If it were true that Lewis and Shantorian were somehow linked, then they'd have the upper hand. Who knew what Lewis had put in place at the hangar while we weren't paying attention? If he had turned on us, or worse, was against us from the start, then he could also be a lot smarter than we thought he was. The possibilities were endless and scary, but what could we do? Lewis was out there, we'd lost track of him, and we didn't know whose side he was on.

Lazlo left final instructions for us, then he got in his car and headed off to the biggest meeting of his life. He would bring Shantorian to us. It was on us to be ready.

Zara went back to her private room and went over everything, checking in with me several times over the next half hour and encouraging me to do the same. She was such a workhorse, and so talented. It occurred to me then that she had become the fourth member of the Trackers. She'd taken Lewis's place, and it felt okay. We sure couldn't hope for anyone with a better work ethic or more skills, and I felt a sense of excitement about what the Trackers could do in the future. The four of us—me, Finn, Emily, and Zara—could do almost anything. Catching Shantorian was just the beginning.

**Tell me about the last few minutes, before they arrived. What was everyone doing?**

I was at the Vault checking over every camera link, sending feeds to Emily and Finn on their monitors. Zara was stationed in her private office, where Shantorian couldn't see her. She'd monitor everything he did in the Vault once he activated the Raymond disk. Emily and Finn were both stationed in the hangar, cycling through different camera views and checking in on wireless mics. Emily had some trouble with the Trinity going all static on her and raced into the Vault with minutes to spare.

"Why is it doing that?" she asked. It was as if some sort of frequency-jamming device were at play. Looking up, I realized that some of the other cameras were failing.

"Uh-oh," I remember saying. "Something's not right."

Cameras were going haywire all over the place. I tried the feed into Zara's room but got nothing but fuzz. Cycling through the outside cameras gave me zero feed.

We were blind.

"Finn!" I yelled "Get outside with your Belinski and keep an eye on the driveway!"

"On that!" he shouted back, on his board and out the door.

Some of the pure Trackers devices, the ones I'd built myself, seemed to still deliver critical images to the Vault. The Trinity was shaky, but at least it was offering up occasional data. The weird thing was that the Belinski, the simplest camera of them all, seemed to be working fine.

**I guess that goes to show you, sometimes simple is best.**

You said it. Every other camera in and outside the hangar—all forty-three of them—failed. Someone had hacked into the wireless grid and shut us down. There was a creepy, electric hum hanging in the air.

Then the lights went out.

Power was being cut everywhere, but the Vault was lit up like a Christmas tree with fuzzy screens.

I yelled for Emily to get up onto a catwalk where it was safe, but she wouldn't budge.

"The Trinity still works," she said. "I can still record with it. I'll feed you what I can."

Her camera still fed scratchy images into the Vault, and Finn's Belinski remained all systems go. They were the only two live monitors. I yelled for Zara, but she either couldn't hear me or was too focused on trying to keep the wheels on with her own challenges to answer.

I did my best to play the part I had always played: the leader of the Trackers. I told Emily to start working on some sort of cover so she could stay in the room with me and record what was going on without being seen. Then I told Finn to get back inside the moment he got a visual on Lazlo returning with Shantorian. I'd have to find a place to put him, too, and I was trying to figure that out when I looked at the Vault monitor, and sure enough, right on time, Finn had a visual.

A light was coming up the long drive, dim and slow. It struck me then that we might really be in danger. What if Shantorian had taken out Lazlo and was walking up the drive, flashlight in hand? Or maybe he was on a motorcycle. Either way, we were in BIG trouble. The hangar was compromised, and it appeared we might be getting a visit from Shantorian without Lazlo there to help us. This was bad.

**It sounds as if Shantorian had you right where he wanted you.**

It sure felt that way. And just as importantly, it was becoming obvious to us all that Lewis had betrayed us. Now I knew what he'd been doing all those lost hours: rigging up his own hacks into the hangar system of cameras and computers.

Something about the idea of Shantorian showing up without Lazlo there to help scared me half to death. I tried to find Emily, but she'd hidden herself surprisingly well. I called her name, but she didn't answer.

Finn piped in from outside, "I have a visual — you getting this?"

"Yeah, I got it — get back in here!" I told him. "We're regrouping!"

I yelled for Emily again but she wouldn't answer.

She was gone.

## What do you mean, *gone*?

I mean Emily wasn't in the room anymore.

I turned to the back wall in the Vault and there she was, her face on one of the monitors.

"Emily, where are you?" I asked her. I was surprised she'd gone off on her own without telling me. She opened her mouth to speak, but Finn threw open the door before she could answer.

"He's coming in!" Finn warned. "And way too fast!"

I braced myself for my first look at Shantorian, more scared than I'd ever been in my life. From the sound of it, this guy was planning a grand entrance, something to really rattle us and put us on our heels. In the light of fuzzed-out monitors in the Vault, something on two wheels blasted through the doorway. It wasn't until he slammed on the brakes and wiped out into the Vault that I realized it wasn't Shantorian.

It was Lewis.

I was fighting mad at that point and I really laid into him. "Lewis! Get your bike out of my Vault! What's wrong with you? And while I'm at it, where have you been?"

Emily was still on the monitor, a miracle since Lewis's bike had sent sparks flying, knocking out power to half the Vault.

"Adam," she said, "calm down."

"Don't tell me to calm down! Shantorian's going to show up any second with Lazlo, and then what? And while we're at it, I'm tired of you always taking his side. Why don't you take *my* side for a change? Lewis is about to wreck the biggest mission of our lives. How can you not see that? Don't you even care?"

Emily calmly replied from some secret place in the hangar. "Oh, we care, Adam. Trust me, we care."

## Something's not right about this scene. What was really going on?

I told everyone to get back into position, but no one moved. Lewis stared at the floor but wouldn't pick up his stupid bike. But Finn was looking right at me. Sometimes, when it really mattered, he could level me with a stare. This was one of those times.

"You gotta trust us, Adam," Finn said. "There's no time to explain. We just gotta get out of here, like, right now."

"You've all gone insane!" I yelled. "Get back to your positions and get this bike out of my Vault!"

Emily spoke next, and what she said nearly took my legs out from underneath me.

"We're leaving, Adam. If you don't want to come with us, that's your call. It's all about trust, right? This is your chance to put the Trackers back together again. Trust us. We know what we're doing."

Lewis was gone in a flash, out into the hangar, where he

must have expected to find Emily. Finn stopped when he got to me, all business. He motioned up to the Vault screens, which had all come back online. Whoever had hacked the system had decided to put all the cameras back to work again.

I saw what Finn wanted me to see.

Headlights, coming up the long driveway to the hangar.

"They're coming," Finn said. "You don't want to be here when that door opens."

Lazlo and Shantorian were about to show up, and these guys wanted out. Everything about the situation told me they'd lost their nerve, ready to run at the crucial moment. Maybe I only *thought* I'd trained up a crack team of Trackers. Maybe, when push came to shove, they were too chicken for anything that might risk their futures.

But there was another part of me, a bigger part, that told me something very different. These were my friends, and that mattered more to me than anything else. If we had to run, then we'd run, but we'd do it together.

"Okay, Finn," I said, "but you better know what you're doing. Grab Zara—I'm getting some equipment."

Emily was back on her monitor again, yelling at me from the front seat of the golf cart.

"Just leave it, Adam, we have to go. Now!"

But I didn't listen. Whatever happened, there was no way I was leaving the most important stuff behind. I dumped over a plastic bin of motherboards. Ten seconds later I'd filled the bin with flash drives full of code, cameras, hard drives, controllers, all my most important tools, my soldering gun, notebooks, a stack of portable batteries—it all went in as I yelled for Zara. The one thing I couldn't find was probably the most important thing.

**The Raymond disk.**

You guessed it. At that moment, I had no idea where it was. Maybe Lewis had taken it while I wasn't watching—he was proving craftier than I'd ever expected. Or Emily. She'd been in the Vault with me. Even Finn had been hanging around during the past hour, a time frame for which I couldn't completely account for the Raymond disk.

At that moment, I seriously didn't know who I could trust.

The monitor showed headlights pulling up to the door as I raced through the hangar.

"We can't just leave her behind!" I yelled. Finn, Lewis, and Emily pulled up beside me and dropped the bin in the back of the cart. Without any warning at all, Lewis grabbed me by my shirt collar and yelled for Emily to gun it, which she did.

I was literally being dragged along the slick floor until I caught a foothold and jumped on board.

If I was mad before, now I was ready to scream at these guys, but I just looked back in the direction of the Vault as Emily drove through the dark, headlights off, toward the far back end of the hangar.

I couldn't believe they'd stoop so low, leaving Lazlo and

Zara to deal with Shantorian alone. Did they care about the Trackers so much that they'd trash ISD and everything Lazlo had worked for all his life?

I didn't speak. No one did. The far back garage door to the hangar was open and we slipped out into the night in total silence.

**Why did they run, Adam?**

We drove in the darkness for, I don't know, a few miles before anyone spoke. The nice thing about a golf cart is that it's quiet. We used side roads, kept the lights off. At some point Finn couldn't stand it anymore.

"Show us what you got, Lewis," he said.

"Can you stop the cart, so we can all watch?" Lewis replied.

I was like, what the heck are you guys even talking about?

"You're sure, then?" Emily asked, pulling down a side street where there were no streetlights.

A few seconds later, I heard Lewis say the same words I'd heard from Zara not that long ago: "Prepare to have your minds blown."

Lewis fired up the Deckard, its small screen coming to life with a video that glowed in all our faces.

**Let me guess. You have that video and you want to present it as evidence?**

We can't go on until you see what Lewis shared with us that night. It's a real showstopper.

**Okay then, load it up.**

*Note: A transcript of this video appears in Appendix P, page 148.*

www.trackersinterface.com

PASSWORD

RALPHBAER

**I imagine even you were at a loss for words after watching that surveillance footage.**

No doubt.

**Let me recap what we just saw, so I'm sure I understand. The Trackers went rogue on you. They saw you were being pulled under Lazlo's spell, but they didn't trust him. So Lewis, Emily, and Finn made a plan of their own. They didn't pick up the camera at the bank, even if Lazlo thought they did. They showed Lazlo the dummy version, the one Lewis used to practice with.**

If Lewis and Emily had removed the camera, we never would have known for sure who took the money. Those codes gave Lazlo the ability to complete phase one of stealing billions. The video proves he did it.

**I wouldn't go that far. All we see is a bank manager getting very nervous. There's no way to tie Lazlo to what happened. It might just as easily have been you and your friends. In fact, that seems more likely.**

It's incredibly hard to prove something to you. Has anyone ever told you that?

**All the time.**

Let's assume for the moment that Lazlo *did* move the money. It wouldn't matter. He still couldn't steal it, not yet.

**But I thought you said he stole the money.**

No, I said he *moved* the money. I realize this is hard to grasp. The digital world often is for people of your advanced age.

**Now you're getting personal. I'm only thirty-six. They haven't put me in a nursing home yet.**

Think about it as if a bank account is a plastic garbage bag. The bag is stuffed full of money and you're standing outside on a windy day. Open the bag and let the money go — that's what those codes did for Lazlo. Small amounts of money from tens of thousands of accounts were flying around all over the place, loose in the system, but he couldn't put it all in a different bag without someone seeing him do it.

**Are you telling me billions of dollars were just floating around? Very hard to believe.**

Listen, trillions of dollars change hands every hour in the world banking system. A few billion is nothing in the overall scope of things. Lazlo had *access* to a lot of money; he could complete the transaction when he was ready, but it would require something more to put that money into his own bags and get away unseen. Someone would have to push the red button.

**The Internet would need to be completely shut down.**

That's right. The whole system asleep, one guy connecting dots and slipping away undetected.

At that point I could only guess Lazlo had the power to pull it off. But I wasn't positive. Either he had taken the Raymond disk or someone else had, because I couldn't find it when we left the hangar.

It's a good thing it wasn't armed or you'd be short several billion bucks.

**But I thought —**

Yeah, you thought. *Everyone* thought. My friends included. But you know what? I wasn't as dazzled by Lazlo as everyone assumed I was. And I've always been one to have a backup plan, just in case.

**This is getting interesting.**

Oh, I have your attention, do I?

**Tell me about this backup plan of yours. But first, where's Shantorian in all of this? He seems to have disappeared into thin air, as he always does.**

You're not getting it at all. I expected more from a high-level agent such as yourself.

**Flattery will get you nowhere.**

Listen, Lieutenant Ganz —

**Calling me by my name finally? How pleasant to be taken seriously for a change.**

Whatever — just listen to what I'm saying. There is no Shantorian. There never has been. You've been chasing a shadow and so have we. It was always Lazlo. He created the world of ISD, the character of Shantorian, all of it. And he did it so we'd open all the doors for him and point all the evidence to ourselves.

Zara was a programming prodigy, but even she couldn't program the Raymond disk to shut down the Internet on her own. She needed my help. Those parts of the code that came from Shantorian? They came from *Zara*. All the game solves, the videos from Shantorian, everything else — those were all an elaborate hoax to keep me programming while Lazlo pinned all the evidence on us.

**I'd say he did a pretty good job. All the evidence *does* point to you.**

I'm not finished yet.

**I thought as much. By the time this is over, it will be Finn who has the money hidden in his skateboard helmet.**

It would be tough hiding a fortune in there. His head would have to be the size of a hot air balloon.

**Where was Zara in this scenario?**

She was recruited, just like we were. Only she was in a lot deeper. She went along willingly, but don't forget her back-story. No family, a street kid. Lazlo knew how to push her buttons right up to the part where the money disappeared. He played us perfectly. When it came to father figures, I think Zara had a weak spot.

**Oh, one more thing before we move on to this backup plan of yours. We both know who was driving up in that car at the hangar, don't we?**

Yes we do. I can even show you. Would you like to see it?

**I would.**

*Note: A transcript of this video appears in Appendix Q, page 151.*

www.trackersinterface.com

PASSWORD

# SERGEYSTEVEMARK

You look better in person. And the camera is especially unkind to Lieutenant Marks. That dude isn't nearly as ugly in person.

**Very funny. As you can see from your own footage, we went through every room and every file in the hangar and nothing indicated the existence of anyone called Lazlo or Zara. There was a lot of evidence, all of it pointing to you and your friends. These videos you keep showing me? That's *your* evidence, and knowing you and your friends, it's been manufactured to get you off the hook.**

Like I said, I'm not finished yet.

**Do please continue. I'm on the edge of my seat.**

Lewis had been busy during all that downtime at the hangar, and he was gone a lot more than I realized. I was so immersed in the work I was doing I really didn't pay attention, and I don't think Zara or Lazlo did, either. As far as they were concerned, Lewis was a harmless liability.

Emily and Finn were in on it from the start, and it turns out they were doing a great job of providing cover for Lewis. Sometimes we all thought he was playing video games or out running around with Finn and Emily—that's what they told us—but Lewis wasn't even in the hangar, especially at night when I was busy working.

"I was gone for six or seven hours at a whack," Lewis told me. "Nobody even noticed, which is kind of sad now that I think about it."

We ditched the golf cart on a side street and boarded a bus into downtown Seattle. I kept asking Lewis where we were going, but he wouldn't say. He also wouldn't talk about everything that had happened. No one would. I tried, at one point, to say I was sorry, but Emily put up her hand and said, "Save it."

Talk about a long bus ride. It felt like we'd hit bottom. Trust had been smashed apart, we were totally implicated in the crime of the century, and we had no place to go. It was the lowest point for me in all of this.

**So you went home?**

No, not home, unless you consider the roof of the Green Lantern home. It was Finn's idea, mostly because he was in love with the idea of skating as late as he wanted to while the rest of us worked into the night.

**You're referring to the private indoor half-pipe Finn had access to? We did some background on that facility. Turns out it's owned by one of Finn's friends, a Mr. Tewfik, retired from Microsoft at the ripe old age of twenty-nine with about fifty million.**

Yeah, Tewfik loves skating—at least that's what Finn says. Nice to have friends in high places, I guess. Finn begged us to let him stop in for a few minutes of serious skating while no one was around. Midnight at the Green Lantern on a weeknight was empty, which was just what Finn wanted: the whole thing to himself. He'd have to wait until we were settled in and had a chance to talk, but skating was close at hand, and that put him in a great mood.

We used Finn's access number to get in, then Lewis took the lead and guided us to another locked door at the far end of the half-pipe.

"My lock-picking skills really came in handy here," Lewis told us.

Within a few seconds, Finn had the door open and we were heading up a dark set of graffiti-filled stairs. The building that houses the Green Lantern is seven or eight stories high, but the skating area only takes up the first two floors. All the upper floors are trashed and empty, and Tewfik isn't interested in remodeling. He's holding the property for the real estate value and the skating, nothing else. So basically the building is abandoned unless you happen to be part of an exclusive gang of skaters.

I was amazed to discover how much work Lewis had done on the top floor. The windows had been boarded, but he'd opened things up in the corner so we could see into the night sky. It was like a fort up there, overlooking the bay on one side and the lights of the city on the other.

"Dang, Lewis, you done good. *Real* good," Finn said when he saw it. "We could live up here."

And he was right. Lewis had set up tables and power cords, sleeping bags, a crate of junk food, a case of Mountain Dew, and two laptops. One of them was wired into the hangar, where we'd set up almost forty cameras, and Lewis directed us to take a look. While we were gone, he'd recorded the scene I already showed you, where you and your goons crashed the hangar.

When I saw you guys enter Zara's room and realized it was empty, I was devastated.

"Where'd she go?" I asked. "And *why'd* she go?"

We all sat down, staring out over the open water. It felt like the Trackers were ready to talk, so I started.

"You guys," I said, "I know I blew it. I didn't trust Lewis. I got sucked into Lazlo's world and lost my focus. I'm sorry."

"We're sorry, too," Lewis told me.

"We are?" Finn asked.

"Yeah, we're sorry, too," Emily said firmly. It was a big deal, because Emily was the toughest of the Trackers. When she was betrayed, she had a hard time letting it go. She went on, and I let her, trying hard not to interrupt.

"We didn't trust you, either, Adam. We could have told you what we were doing, but we didn't. We weren't sure until the very end, but it was wrong for us to go rogue on you like that. We were supposed to trust each other, but when things got really tough, we couldn't hold it together. I'll tell you this much: I wish we'd been wrong. We're in serious trouble here. All the evidence points to us. As far as the cops are concerned, it looks like we opened those banks. Actually, we kind of *did* open those banks. According to Lewis, there's a lot of money missing."

"How much?" I asked.

Lewis handed me a slip of paper with calculations on it.

"It's not complete," he said. "But I think it's close. Four billion and change."

**The actual figure, if you want to know, is $4,300,200,100. A poetic number, wouldn't you say?**

That's a lot of zeros.

**Enough to get you and your friends tried as adults.**

Hold on a second—you never said that!

**I'm saying it now. The sun's coming up, Adam. It's a new day, the first of what I'm guessing will be a minimum of ten years behind bars. Say good-bye to your childhood. It's over.**

I guess this means you still don't believe me.

**The money is missing; you took it. Even Emily said so. Thanks for that testimony; it will be very helpful.**

Hold on, that's not what I said... not what *she* said. Just let me finish and you'll see.

**I'm waiting.**

The big question that remained for all of us was whether or not we should go on without getting help. Finn was up for anything, as long as we did it together and never distrusted each other again. Emily and Lewis were leaning toward calling our parents, telling them the entire story, and taking our chances with the authorities. I had to admit I was scared, but I wasn't even close to being ready to give up.

And I had an ace up my sleeve, something I hadn't told anyone. I was a little nervous about mentioning it, because we'd restored trust within the Trackers and it might be seen as a deception.

**Is this your so-called backup plan? It better be good.**

I remember it exactly, because I'd thought about how to tell them during the long silence on the bus ride over.

This is how I explained it to my team:

"I didn't tell you guys everything I was working on. I wish I had, but I didn't. The truth is I didn't think I'd ever *need* to tell anyone. It was just a precaution, in case everything came unglued like before. It wasn't that I didn't trust Lazlo, because I did. It's just part of who I am, always creating a way out in case things get too crazy."

"This oughta be good," Finn said. He was sitting on his board, wobbling back and forth in anticipation.

"The Raymond disk is a very particular sort of device," I explained. "You guys didn't spend a lot of time with it, but

I did. When we got it from Lazlo, it was just a chip, remember? Back then the Raymond chip didn't really work as advertised, it was all smoke and mirrors, a way to draw us into ISD."

**So according to your version, the Raymond device could show you things, but it didn't give you the ability to take them. Is that it?**

Bingo. We could see inside the banks and the first level of classified intelligence, but that was it. If we'd touched anything, we'd have been caught, and Lazlo knew that. He also knew that if he could put me and Zara on it together, we could crack the code.

**You could take what was essentially an artifact and arm it.**

And that's exactly what we did. We armed the Raymond device.

**This doesn't sound like much of a backup plan.**

Funny, that's exactly what the Trackers said. I had to remind them that when we first came into contact with the Raymond device, it was only a microchip, nothing else. I built the casing for it, remember? And if you'll recall, there were three small light diodes on one end: green, yellow, red. Green for banks, yellow for intel, red for shutting down the Internet. The whole thing looked like a portable flash drive, nothing special. But I was a lot more nervous about Lazlo and Zara back then than I was at the hangar. There was no trust between us. In fact, I was sure they were criminals.

**Funny how getting to know people will change your feelings about them.**

I had every reason to include a safeguard, a way to get out of trouble if the Raymond disk ended up in the wrong hands.

**So what did you do?**

I hot-wired it.

**I'm not following.**

Let's take this back into the building we were hiding out in, because I want to make sure to include how everyone responded. It's important, so just bear with me.

"Have you ever seen one of those movies where someone tries to defuse a bomb?" That's the question I asked Emily, Finn, and Lewis.

Finn got it immediately.

"Like when they have to cut the wires in just the right order or the whole place goes BOOM!" he said.

I nodded and said, "I sort of did the same thing with the Raymond disk. There were three wire connections inside the flash drive casing, but you had to unscrew the top in order to see them. There was no reason to get into the guts of the device, because you simply plugged it into a USB port and it worked. Whatever computer you stuck it into was armed. Zara and I passed it back and forth from time to time, loading new code onto it, but generally speaking, it was locked up in the Vault with me. There were a couple of times when I went looking for it and found it missing. I'd ask Zara and it was always accounted for, she was loading code onto it or testing that everything was fine. But something didn't feel right. What if she was using it for something else?"

Emily asked what we were all thinking: "Like opening up the banks for real, using those access codes we helped them get, and draining billions out of accounts?"

And I wrapped up what I needed to tell them. "Yesterday was total chaos. Everyone was running around doing something, so it provided the perfect opportunity for me to tinker with the Raymond disk. I unscrewed the top, where the three light diodes were, and disconnected the three wires. And here's the thing about those wires: One was red, one was blue, and one was white. But I'd programmed it so that a few clicks of the mouse would arm the Raymond disk in a different way: self-destruct. I plugged it into my laptop, ran a quick program I'd written, and it was ready to go."

"I like the sound of this so far," said Lewis. "It's devious, but tricky."

"Those are the same thing," Emily said.

"Exactly." Lewis smiled at that one. So did I, because it felt like the Trackers were back. They weren't mad at me for holding out on them; they were psyched as all get-out that we still had a chance, and it showed on everyone's face.

My big finale went like this:

"So here's how it works: If Lazlo tries to use the Raymond disk again, it won't do anything. He's already got the money out of the accounts, but he has to push the red button in order to move the money where he wants without being detected. Probably Zara will figure out it's been disarmed, open it up, and see the loose wires. If she's smart, which of course she is, she'll realize that wiring it back up might be a bad idea. Maybe I switched the colors around. Maybe blue goes with red now. And maybe, just maybe, if you wire it up wrong, the Raymond disk self-destructs."

"But you can't have expected her to realize all that," Emily said.

"True," I told her. "That's why I put a message inside the casing on a tiny piece of paper so she couldn't miss it."

"Old-school! I like it." Finn always has the right thing to say.

I figured if Shantorian really did show up, I could reverse the program and rewire the Raymond disk in front of everyone. It would show I'd thought ahead, put in a safety net. What would be the harm?

This is what the note I put with the disk said: *Wrong order = self-destruct. Rearm at your own risk.* Then I gave them a special e-mail account I'd created for this one purpose. If someone wanted to talk, they knew where to find me.

**Very clever, Adam. You might make a believer out of me yet.**

During the next hour or so, Finn went skating, we all ate too much junk food, and I did some work on the Trinity and the Deckard so they were in tip-top shape. Emily and Lewis set up some of the equipment I'd brought from the Vault, and I had them start compiling evidence. Lewis is our best video guy, so he hunkered down on the evidence we'd already recorded.

**Did he create most of the evidence you've been showing me all night?**

You got it. He turned out to be a lot more important than even I gave him credit for, and I made sure he knew it. The guy is amazing.

**Assuming this is all true, I'm hoping Lazlo tried to contact you.**

He did.

**Do tell.**

Better if I show you. For once we had him where we wanted him, or so we thought.

*Note: A transcript of this video appears in Appendix R, page 153.*

www.trackersinterface.com

PASSWORD

# NIMDA

**Your story gets more interesting by the minute.**

Thank you, I do try.

**Tell me, though, if Lazlo is the criminal you say he is, why has he put so much evidence against himself in your hands? Kind of careless for a mastermind, wouldn't you agree?**

I suppose it depends on your point of view. True, he's all over these recordings, but he also has a red button of his own if you'll recall. He had all my inventions—the Deckard, the Trinity, the Orville, and the Belinski—and he could still release all the plans to whomever he wanted. But more than that, he knew there was plenty of evidence against us piled up in the hangar.

**He was right about that. Minus your story and these videos you've been showing me, everything still points to you and the Trackers. And there's still the matter of the missing money.**

I think the real reason he took those risks was because he misread who I was.

**Explain what you mean.**

107

Lazlo is a master of manipulation. At the hangar, he never stopped telling me how talented I was. I remember one late night in the Vault. It was just me and him, no one else around, and he said all the things I needed to hear.

"There's something special about you, Adam. These things you've made will change the world. When this is over, you'll see."

Everything Lazlo did was designed to make me see what was important: my own ambitions. The Trackers? A means to an end, nothing more. They couldn't be trusted, and he would show me that. The fact that he had access to everything I'd ever done, every line of code I'd ever written that was any good, all the plans for everything I'd ever created in the Vault — that gave him power over me.

At least that's what he thought.

**But he was wrong?**

It seems to me that a person like Lazlo is either very right or very wrong most of the time. So yes, he was wrong. *Very* wrong. Losing the trust of my friends had made one thing crystal clear to me: They mattered a billion times more than anything I could create on my own. Without them, none of it made any sense. Sure I was ambitious and creative, the perfect one-two punch in the world of technology, but I was a friend first.

Maybe if Lazlo had found me in ten years, after I'd been jaded by the adult world, I'd have fallen more deeply under his deception.

**Under that line of thinking, Zara was what? The anti-Adam? Your evil twin?**

No, that's not right. We all saw her as having fallen under Lazlo's dark spell. She had a much tougher background. She didn't know what else to do but what she was told. If I could have reached her then, I would have. I think I could have turned her in a different direction.

**What happened next, after Lazlo contacted you demanding help?**

We didn't have the Raymond disk, but I'd used it to gain access to at least some intel. I couldn't go very deep, but I could get deep enough to listen in on FBI chatter between cell phones. It's an area that's still a little loose with the rules. I hacked into the system far enough to gain access to mid-level agents, and put Finn to work.

**That's a federal offense.**

I wasn't selling secrets to another country; I was simply trying to ascertain how widely the bank debacle was known.

**I'm simply keeping you informed of your infractions, of which there are many.**

If you're trying to rattle me, it's working.

**Good. What did you discover by hacking into FBI cell phones?**

Well, for starters, those guys text a lot. Finn was swimming in tens of thousands of data points, but Lewis ran some sweet filters that narrowed things down into the thousands. This is an area where Finn is talented, and it really showed that night. It's kind of weird, but Finn has one of those brains where you can put a lot of information in front of him and he can find a pattern.

"Finally, something I'm good at—bring it on." That's how Finn responded to a scrolling screen of text messages. His eyes danced over the screen, watching as messages came through, dozens of them a second. The filter made it so he only saw posts that had the words *bank*, *money*, or *hacked* in them, but it was still a huge amount of data.

"Got one," Finn would yell every few minutes, and we'd tag a relevant post. After about a half hour Finn had a hundred or so posts that gave us a critical piece of information.

**Which was?**

The pattern was clear: Only the bank presidents were aware that anything was going on, them and the FBI. There was real concern that the information stay locked down for fear of a run on the banks. If a story ran online about billions of dollars unaccounted for and a systemwide hack, there was a real chance businesses and private account holders would freak out. The whole financial system could collapse.

"This is good," I remember Lewis saying. "It hasn't gone wide."

"Yeah, but how long can something like this stay secret?" Emily asked. "I bet we have a day, maybe two at most, and the whole world is going to know."

Finn snapped his fingers a few times, as if to tell us he was seeing something.

"Whoa, how do you stop this thing? I need to scroll back," he said. While we were talking, the screen had been scrolling new texts, and one of them had caught Finn's eye.

Lewis typed out some commands on the laptop, and scrolled slowly back up the screen until Finn yelled, "There! That's the one."

Emily said what we were all feeling: "Finn, you're amazing."

"Don't I know it," he replied.

**What did Finn discover?**

Someone was posing as an FBI agent, probably had been for a long time.

The FBI has a mole, and his name?

Lazlo.

**If what you're saying is true, it's a major breach of national security.**

That's *your* problem. I've got a four-billion-dollar problem of my own. But it's true. And the message was a warning. It was the signature that got us.

*Do we have an Adam Henderson in the database? O_o*

**Weird-faced kid. Shantorian's signature.**

You got it. Chances are he sent the text to a low-level flunky who didn't know about Shantorian, but the text was for me. He was calling me out, letting me know if I wasn't careful, he'd start connecting the dots for the FBI.

**That Finn has got some talent.**

Mad skills, no doubt. We lifted the number Lazlo texted from and used it to open a line of communication. I had a message for him as well.

*I'm ready to push the red button.*

**That must have been an eye-popping text message for Lazlo.**

His text answer was short and sweet:

*I see you are paying attention. I look forward to concluding our business.*

So we were set. Ten o'clock the next night and it was game on. Either Lazlo would walk with the money, or we'd have to figure out a way to stop him.

**By my calculations, this meeting took place at the county fair two nights ago. Is that correct?**

Exactly, and that location was going to be a big problem. Lazlo chose well. With so many people milling around and all that noise from the rides and the vendors, it would be all too easy for Lazlo to slip away once he got what he wanted.

We were all exhausted, and together we decided if we were going to get any sleep, we'd better get it quick. We needed to do some planning and double-check all the equipment. But if there was one thing I'd learned from taking finals at school it was this: Sleep matters. Our brains were turning to mush, like we'd pulled an all-nighter studying. We'd pushed it as far as we could.

Sleep is a funny thing to me, kind of like dying and then coming back to life again. And this particular round of sleep was about as much like death as it had ever been. We're talking super-deep sleep, the kind that an alarm set on your cell phone has no impact on.

**You overslept?**

Yeah, we overslept. The windows were mostly boarded up so it was pretty dim in there, and before I knew it, it was after two and I was hearing Emily yelling for me to get up.

But it was good, because we were alert and focused. We figured out what everyone was going to do, talked through the plan, and I think you know what happened next.

**You texted me.**

At six o'clock sharp.

**Which reminds me — how did you even get my number?**

You were on your phone in the hangar. We had a lot of cameras in there, some of them Deckard hybrids.

**Superzoom.**

You guessed it. There was a moment where you dialed a number. We ran a trace, figured out who you were contacting. The rest was pretty easy, since we had access to time stamps and calling activity.

**Have you got any idea how many laws you've broken in the past few days? Your only chance for survival in the real world is turning up that money. All other options are a dead end.**

And here I thought we were starting to get along. Guess I was wrong.

**I've got a copy of the text you sent me right here. It said: *It's me, Adam Henderson. Missing something?***

Yeah, that was a good one. You think?

I'm not even going to answer that. We had your name from a night and day of gathering evidence in the hangar.

My reply to you: *Don't play games. Turn yourself in.*

Your answer back: *Keep your phone handy. I'll contact you when it's time.*

My reply: *Time for what?*

Your answer: *Time to get your money back.*

You didn't respond to any of my messages after that, but I did get one more text at nine o'clock, an hour before your meeting. You could have made it easier on me.

But then I wouldn't have taken you seriously. Come on, it wasn't that hard.

Your message to me: *47°11'00.08"N, 122°17'46.29"W,* coordinates for the fairgrounds.

I know, we were busy.

I'm going to guess you have another video to show me of that night.

That I do. *House of mirrors*, as it's come to be known within our small ranks. The toughest surveillance assignment the Trackers have ever done.

**And their last.**

If you say so.

*Note: A transcript of this video appears in Appendix S, page 157.*

www.trackersinterface.com

PASSWORD

**HAL9000**

How did you know where we were? It's not like we told you what we were doing.

**You're not the only one doing surveillance, Adam. And who knows, maybe I've got a few tricks of my own. Ever think of that?**

Honestly, I don't think you have a tricky bone in your body. But I've been wrong before.

**Let's stick to the facts of the video you just showed me. Run it down. What happened?**

What's to tell? You saw the whole thing. Lazlo showed up, I sat down on a bench next to him, we talked. The rest of the Trackers kept an eye on Zara and me from different locations inside the fair. In the end, she slipped away and you caught us. End of story.

**Did you repair the Raymond disk or didn't you?**

No. But as far as Lazlo knew, it sure looked like I'd fixed it. All those numbers flying by on his laptop screen? They had the appearance of money moving into accounts. And it sure looked like the Internet had suddenly gone dark. Lazlo felt that he'd gotten what he'd come for, but in reality, I'd just released a potent virus onto his laptop.

## A virus that infected just one computer — Lazlo's?

Poetic justice. In the beginning, he and Zara had tricked me with the Glyphmaster by making me think thousands of people were playing it online. But I was the only one who could even see it. What Lazlo was seeing on his laptop screen at the fair was confined to him and him alone. For him, the Internet *had* shut down. Money really *was* moving into his accounts. The digital world really *had* come to an end. Too bad for Lazlo there was only one place where these truths existed: in the tiny world of his own computer.

## Impressive.

Impressive? I wish. Lazlo is probably in Russia by now while my friends and I are being blamed for the crime of the century. Seems to me, in the end, we failed.

Just tell me one thing — how did you know exactly where we were at that fair? The coordinates I sent to your phone only got you to the front gate, in case we needed you.

## We were tipped off.

Tipped off? By who? Wait, don't answer that. He's an even bigger jerk than I thought he was. He set us up. Unbelievable.

**Yes, Lazlo is quite the criminal mastermind. Let me show you something you might not have expected.**

*I turned to the double mirror and signaled. Our best chance of recovering the funds would be right now.*

**Adam, prepare to have your mind blown yet again.**

Good luck with that, there's nothing you could—

*Let the record show that Lazlo has been escorted into the room and seated across from Adam Henderson.*

Lazlo: Hello, Adam. Always a pleasure to see you.

Adam: No way.

**Bring the rest of them in.**

Lazlo: You and your friends turned out to be more trouble than I expected.

Adam: Sorry to disappoint you.

*Emily, Lewis, and Finn have entered the room with armed escorts. I've sat them down in three chairs along one side of the table. I sit across from them. Adam and Lazlo are facing each other, staring each other down. No one is speaking. I remove the Raymond disk from my pocket and place it on the table between them.*

**Adam, it's time to rearrange some ones and zeros. Find the money, put it back where it belongs, and no one will ever know it was missing.**

Adam: Tell us one thing first. Where's Zara?

Lazlo: May I answer that? It's the least you can allow me.

**Fine, but make it quick. I've got a schedule to keep.**

Lazlo: Adam, you and your friends here, you mistrusted the wrong person. I was never the mastermind of our little game. There's only one person not in this room right now, and she's the only one who *should* be here.

Emily: Zara? You're telling us Zara was in charge?

Lazlo: She recruited *me*, not the other way around. Zara is more than simply brilliant—she's more akin to an evil genius. Everything you went through was devised by her. I only followed instructions, for a small piece of the final take. When she saw her plan was going to fail, she cut her losses. You see, in Zara's world I was a dispensable asset, same as you.

Her real ambition has never faltered: to kill the Internet.

Adam: But why would anyone want to do that?

Lazlo: How does the old saying go, the one about climbing the big mountain? Because it's there. Your grandfather was a legendary mountain man, you should understand that.

Adam: I see what you mean. For someone of Zara's skills and ambition, the Internet would be the ultimate digital mountain.

Finn: Yeah, but it sounds like she wasn't trying to climb it.

Emily: She was trying to knock it down.

Lazlo: You Trackers, always so dramatic. The truth of the matter is simple: Zara tricked you. She tricked me. And she got away.

Adam: Is that true? Is she really missing?

**Zara, Shantorian, Raymond — she goes by many names. And yes, she's vanished into thin air. It's not the first time. This girl has been giving us trouble for years. The fact that we came so close to catching her this time tells**

**us one thing: She let her guard down. She's never done that before.**

Adam: Maybe she really needed the money.

Lazlo: Oh, I don't think so, Adam. I think Zara got a taste of what it might have been like to have friends. She saw what you four had and she wanted it for herself. There was something about you that made her think twice. It made her reckless. But in the end, she was the same old Zara—cool, calculating, elusive. No one will ever catch her, not unless she wants to be caught.

**I'd like to think I'll prove you wrong, but I have my doubts.**

**Now, Adam, there is the matter of the missing funds. Those billions of bills are still flying around out there, missing from thousands of accounts where they belong. Do me the service of putting things back in place, won't you?**

Lazlo: I wouldn't if I were you, Adam. Not without some assurances. This agent has plenty of evidence to put us all away for a very long time.

Adam: What do you say, Agent Ganz? If I can make billions of dollars magically appear where they're supposed to be, will you look the other way and let us all walk?

**You're not going anywhere. That's not an option.**

Lazlo: How unfortunate for me.

Emily: What about us?

*Let the record show I made the call and cleared the Trackers for agency exit. The Trackers are all minors, and it will be hard to try them as adults. Plus, we're in a gray area for holding them overnight. Lazlo we can bargain with, keep him quiet. He's looking at a dozen years, minimum. Him I can work with. Maybe he can even be of some use.*

**Promise not to become a problem for me later, and I'll let you go. But so help me, if a single Tracker turns to hacking, I'll track you *all* down. And I'm holding on to every shred of evidence I've collected in the past few days. One false move and you can all kiss your freedom good-bye. Understood?**

Adam: Guys? What do you say?

Finn: I say let's go skating and get a pizza.

Emily: I just want to go home.

Lewis: It's your call, Adam, you're the leader. But I don't see a lot of options here. If she's willing to let us walk, I'd like to have my life back.

Adam: Give me the Raymond disk, my computer tools, and a laptop.

*A few minutes later a box of tools retrieved from the Green Lantern was brought in. Adam called Lewis over and the two of them began working. Within minutes Lewis had the casing off the laptop and Adam had removed the original Raymond chip from the housing. He inserted the chip into the laptop's motherboard and began typing furiously.*

Lazlo: Why does everything have to be so complicated?

Adam: Hey, I didn't invent technology, I just use it. Blame it on your generation.

**Stop talking and focus on the work. I'm starting to doubt you can even do this.**

Adam: No reason to doubt, it's already done. Your precious money is back where it belongs.

Lazlo: How terribly disappointing.

*Traces run, bank funds verified. Mission accomplished. Adam Henderson has put everything back in order.*

*Agent note: This kid scares me. It's not bad enough we have Zara to deal with; I've come to believe Adam is every bit as dangerous. If he turns against us, he's a risk to national security, banks, everything. He and Zara together would be a worldwide digital catastrophe.*

AH: Oh, and Zara left a message on the Raymond disk, in case anyone wants to see it.

EC: Are you serious?

AH: Totally. She must have recorded it prior to the meeting at the fair, just in case things didn't go as she planned. I uploaded it into the interface.

Last piece of video evidence, Agent Ganz. Care to take a look?

*Note: A transcript of this video appears in Appendix T, page 165.*

www.trackersinterface.com

PASSWORD

GRACEHOPPER

## Case close file, end notes.

*Two days have passed.*

*The Trackers were returned to the hangar, where parents were contacted for pickup from TechBase10. As part of a plea bargain, Lazlo played the part of camp host while agents stood on alert inside the hangar. All of Mr. Henderson's mobile technology has been returned to him, along with every part of the Vault. What he will do with these assets in the future concerns me.*

*Zara remains at large. She has completely disappeared and there are no leads worth following. It's as if she never existed.*

*Adam Henderson e-mailed me a letter, which I have included in the file.*

*Case closed, for now.*

Agent Ganz,

I began programming computers when I was too young to realize where it would lead me. Technology took the place of people, until one day I woke up and realized people didn't matter anymore.

I think that's what happened to Zara. I know how she thinks, how it feels to never unplug. Actually, I think a lot of people my age know how Zara feels. You may not realize it, but sometimes we get angry about it. We don't know a world without the Internet and cell phones. And while we love these things, we're also trapped by them. The very idea of letting it all go, of living without having to constantly con-nect, connect, connect—it's an idea some of us dream about.

When you think of Zara, think of our entire gen-eration. In the great sea of technology, there are days when we feel overwhelmed. There are days, now and again, when the idea of getting rid of it all has a certain appeal.

In a way, Zara represents the part of us that wishes we could shut the digital world off. The dif-ference? She has the courage and the brains to make it happen.

Knowing she's out there gives me some hope. Hope that one day I'll roll out of bed and go to my computer or my cell phone like I always do. Only this time, none of it will work. I'll be forced back into the mountains for a good hike, like Old Henderson.

And there I'll find my soul again.

In the meantime, if you need any help, don't hesitate to call me on my cell, text me, e-mail me, try my webcam, or use my handle on any of the major social networking sites.

I never disconnect, so I'm easy to find.

Adam

The following is a transcript of the video shown by Adam Henderson at 02:25 to H. Ganz in Room 214. Transcription and analysis by H. Ganz.

A marker, OPEN VFILE **2640,** indicates some kind of media asset filing system. Below this identifier it reads: PROPERTY OF ADAM HENDERSON **|** DO NOT COPY OR DISTRIBUTE

An image briefly appears of the suspect, Adam Henderson, at his workstation (which he calls "the Vault") in its second location. On-screen text refers to the location as "Vault 2.0."

### Adam

All right, stay focused.

Image switches to a series of stills of the location referred to as "the hangar."

### Adam (voice-over)

We'd moved our operations to the hangar, at ISD, and we had our first major exercise.

Image switches to a map of the area around the hangar.

**Adam (voice-over)**

It was a night surveillance job, and the objective was to get the license number and state from the plates of a car, a black SUV.

*Images of suspects Emily, Lewis, Finn, and Zara appear one by one.*

**Adam (voice-over)**

Emily and Lewis were in a golf cart, and Finn was being pulled behind on his skateboard. Zara was watching from her office. Everyone was in high spirits, and it looked like a slam dunk.

*Image switches to a video feed from the device the suspects refer to as the Deckard, and shows Emily driving a golf cart.*

**Emily**

You know I was born ready.

*Camera shows Lewis riding alongside.*

**Lewis**

Yeah, Adam, we got this!

*Camera shows Finn being pulled behind the golf cart on his skateboard, holding what appears to be a water-ski towline.*

#### Finn

No worries!

*Image switches back to Adam at the Vault.*

#### Adam

All right, I got eyeballs on all the security cams, but it's all about the license plate.

*Shots of Lewis and Emily as an incoming transmission from Zara is indicated on-screen.*

#### Zara (voice transmission)

Remember, you're looking for the plate number *and* the state.

#### ...ily

*...era pans back to Finn being towed behind the ...r cart.*

*Image switches to Adam at the Vault. Suspect appears to be checking various monitors.*

#### Adam

You get anything?

*Image switches to Emily.*

**Emily**

No.

*Camera pans to include the intersection ahead of them just as a dark-colored vehicle speeds across from right to left.*

*Image switches to the Vault.*

**Adam**

Split up. Emily, take the next left hard so Finn shoots straight ahead!

*Image switches to Finn's helmet-mounted camera.*

**(offscreen)**

Letting go at the

*We see an animated map. SUV is
cart in yellow, suspect on skateboard in      red, golf*

**Adam (voice-over)**

With Finn splitting off from the others, it gave us
chance to close in on the vehicle. Finn got there first,
and I guess we all expected to find Lazlo behind the
wheel . . .

*Image switches to Finn's helmet-cam, as he approaches
the SUV, which is empty.*

**Finn (offscreen)**

Are you seeing this?

**Adam (voice-over)**

. . . but there was no one there. As Finn went to see how close the others were, none of us was ready for what happened next.

*Image switches between a security camera showing the parked SUV, Finn on foot, Lewis and Emily in the fast-approaching golf cart, the helmet-cam, and the Deckard, in quick succession, to show the SUV backing up at high speed and impacting the golf cart hard enough to roll it on its side, ejecting the driver and passenger.*

**Finn (offscreen)**

You guys okay?

**Adam (voice-over)**

Finn went to see if someone had gotten back into the car, but it was empty.

*As Finn approaches the car, it takes off at high speed. The Deckard shows Emily standing and brushing herself off as Finn approaches.*

**Emily**

Where's the Trinity?

#### Lewis (offscreen)

Your nose is bleeding.

#### Finn

Let me see?

*Emily touches her nose and sees a small amount of blood on her hand.*

#### Emily

It's nothing. What about you?

*Image switches to Finn's helmet-cam to see Lewis checking his hands and knees, and Emily finding the Trinity on the ground.*

#### Adam (voice-over)

Emily and Lewis were only a little banged up, but I ran out to meet them halfway. That was when we decided to confront Lazlo at the hangar.

*Image switches to a security-camera view inside the hangar that shows the sliding door where the four suspects enter. Someone turns on an extremely bright spotlight, focused directly on them. Adam shields his eyes.*

#### Emily

What are you trying to do, kill us?

**Adam**

That was messed up!

*Image alternates between two security camera images of the group of four, and a feed from the Deckard, held by Lewis.*

**Lazlo (offscreen)**

I think it's the four of *you* who messed up. We're not playing games here, this is the real world. If you can't get a license plate from a remote-controlled vehicle, what chance do you have against Shantorian? I seriously overestimated your tracking skills. Get some sleep.

*The spotlight turns off, leaving the four in near-darkness. As they leave, the image switches to the Deckard, carried by Lewis.*

**Adam**

Man, what have we gotten ourselves into?

**CLOSE VFILE 2640**

The following is a transcript of the video shown by Adam Henderson at 03:33 to H. Ganz in Room 214. Transcription and analysis by H. Ganz.

## OPEN VFILE 2641

*An image of the main branch of Briarcliff Bank appears, then a slow-motion image, in black-and-white, of suspects Adam, Lewis, and Finn in a fifteen-passenger van.*

### Adam (voice-over)

It was time to get the Orville DC installed at the bank. I look back and I realize we were all acting like it was no big deal, that it was just another exercise . . . but it wasn't.

*The image switches to a blueprint of the bank's interior. As Adam describes certain locations, they are highlighted on the floor plan.*

### Adam (voice-over)

The plan had Emily and Lazlo, pretending to be an uncle and his niece, sitting down to talk with the bank manager about moving her ginormous college fund to his branch. During a distraction — that Emily had been rehearsing — we needed to get the Orville DC to the manager's office and into position.

*It's now a four-way security-camera view, all interiors of the bank's main customer area.*

### Adam (voice-over)

We had tapped into the wireless security system at the bank, so we used their own cameras to see how it was going.

*One of the images fills the screen.*

### Adam (voice-over)

Emily is so good at this in-person stuff it's almost scary. And Lazlo . . . sometimes I get the feeling his background involves more covert ops than he lets on.

*Emily is visible as the bank manager speaks with Lazlo. She places a small, light-colored device on the floor next to her bag.*

### Adam (voice-over)

No one saw her get the Orville DC out of her bag, and the distraction worked, so it was up to me to get the unit halfway across the bank without anyone seeing it.

*Image switches to a wireless feed from the Orville DC, rolling along the bank's carpeted floor, past customers' feet, and into the bank manager's office.*

### Adam (voice-over)

If I went too fast, it would make too much noise. But if I went too slow . . . eventually someone's gonna see it.

*Once inside the manager's office, the image switches briefly to a view of Adam, Lewis, and Finn in the van, watching the Orville DC's progress on their devices.*

### Adam

Nice!

*The Orville DC approaches the wall, climbs the base-board, and ascends the wall, turning laterally and driving toward the window. The image switches to a security-camera view of the manager's office, and the Orville DC can be seen "driving" on the wall.*

*The device comes to a stop high on the wall. When it's not moving, the Orville DC closely resembles an infrared motion detector, much like the ones positioned else-where in the bank.*

### Zara (offscreen)

Very nice, guys.

### Adam

You, too, Zara.

*The image transitions to a later version of the same shot; Lazlo and Emily have joined the others, and Adam and Finn appear nearly asleep.*

### Adam (voice-over)

Once it was in place, we had to wait until closing time, and I don't think we were prepared for the wait. There weren't nearly enough snacks, and it didn't seem right to play video games. And then, all of a sudden, it was time.

*Lazlo indicates his watch as he turns to Adam.*

### Lazlo

This is the time when he logs in every day.

*Adam sits up and turns on his device. The image switches to a security-camera view of the bank manager in his office, and then switches again to an image that is apparently sent from the Orville DC, looking over the manager's shoulder as he works at his computer.*

*As he enters a login and password, the image freezes, backs up, then zooms in on the computer screen, undergoing a series of sharpening processes until the text is legible.*

USER ID:  MGR98111
PASSWORD:  B4B4B34R

### Zara (offscreen)

It's definitely clear enough to read here.

*The image switches back to the van, where the suspects congratulate one another. The image freezes and zooms in on Adam's and Finn's fists as they meet.*

### Lazlo (offscreen)

You did good work.

*The image switches to a satellite view of the van in an alley near the bank as it zooms outward and rotates.*

### Adam (voice-over)

We had to hand it to Zara — the Orville DC really delivered. When we were getting ready to leave, I should have noticed that Lewis had to remind Lazlo that we needed to make arrangements to get it back. I just chalked it up to fatigue and didn't think about it again.

*The image switches to the security-camera view of the bank manager's office, slowly zooming into the Orville DC high on the office wall.*

**CLOSE VFILE 2641**

The following is a transcript of the video shown by Adam Henderson at 03:59 to H. Ganz in Room 214. Transcription and analysis by H. Ganz.

### OPEN VFILE 2642

*The image is dark but filled with vertical blue stripes, some kind of digital interference. A computer-generated voice is heard, and a face can barely be seen in the vertical stripes. At times it looks like the image is of someone wearing glasses, and possibly a goatee.*

143

#### Computer-generated voice

What you are doing is very dangerous, and you cannot finish it without me. The intel button has to be unlocked for the plan to work. Of course, the red button will need to be activated as well. To move money around without leaving a trace requires the Internet to be completely nonfunctioning. I will help you if you will listen to me. I'm closer than you think, and I've been watching you. Oh, and one more thing: Someone on your team isn't telling you everything.

*The face fades away and the image is replaced by what appears to be a municipal security camera, location unknown. A figure in a patterned, hooded sweatshirt approaches another figure, dressed in black.*

*As the image zooms in closer, the hooded figure pulls out what appears to be a manila envelope and hands it to the figure in black, who walks away.*

*TRANSCRIBER'S NOTE: Although the identity of the figure in black would be hard to establish conclusively, it appears to be a white male with glasses and some facial hair.*

### Adam (voice-over)

What the heck? Lewis has a meeting that we don't know about?

*The figure in the hooded sweatshirt turns toward the camera and the image freezes and zooms in further.*

*TRANSCRIBER'S NOTE: Although similarly inconclusive, the hooded figure does bear a resemblance to suspect Lewis.*

### Adam (voice-over)

Seeing this footage was like getting punched in the gut. I didn't know what to believe.

*The image switches to a freeze-frame of the digitally obscured face from the beginning of the file.*

### Adam (voice-over)

I had a huge problem, and I didn't have the first idea what to do about it.

**CLOSE VFILE 2642**

The following is a transcript of the video shown by Adam Henderson at 04:27 to H. Ganz in Room 214. Transcription and analysis by H. Ganz.

### OPEN VFILE 2643

*Image is of a young female in near-total darkness.*

*TRANSCRIBER'S NOTE: We can conclusively identify the voice as belonging to Zara.*

### Zara

I'll get right to the point. In order for this to work for everyone involved, we're going to have to meet in person, at the hangar. If we're draining billions of dollars into bank accounts worldwide, it only makes sense that we have to work together and take turns. For a job of this magnitude, we need to plan in person, not just send recorded messages back and forth. Not if we're shutting down intel and actually pressing the red button. Don't you agree?

*The image switches to the digitally concealed suspect who uses the computer-generated voice.*

**Computer-generated voice**

I have attached an encrypted list of banks I claim as mine. The rest are yours. A second encrypted file explains the procedure I've laid out. One bank at a time, but moving quickly enough so the entire procedure takes only a few minutes. You should have no objections. There is a bench at the corner of Broad and John streets. I will wait for you there from 7:45 to 7:50. You drive. Good-bye.

**CLOSE VFILE 2643**

The following is a transcript of the video shown by Adam Henderson at 05:17 to H. Ganz in Room 214. Transcription and analysis by H. Ganz.

**OPEN VFILE 2644**

*Lewis is seen in what appears to be a residential setting, possibly his room at home.*

### Lewis

I have something insanely important to show you.

*The image freezes.*

### Adam (voice-over)

Lewis was right, both about it being important and about it being insane.

*The image switches to the footage already seen in the van outside the bank, as the five suspects are preparing to leave.*

### Adam (voice-over)

Remember that moment in the van, between him and Lazlo? The moment I didn't think much about? Well, because he's Lewis, he thought about it a *lot*.

*The image switches to the security-camera view of the Orville DC on the bank manager's office wall.*

#### Adam (voice-over)
Instead of getting the Orville DC *out* of the bank, he *used* it. To check up on something.

*The image switches to the view from the Orville DC of the bank manager at his computer.*

#### Adam (voice-over)
This was when we started to piece together what Lazlo was *really* up to.

*The image begins to zoom in on the computer monitor and sharpen as before.*

TOTAL MONETARY ASSETS — $0.00

*The bank manager reaches for his phone and makes a call.*

#### Bank manager
Somebody has hacked into the system! No, I haven't told anyone. I called you first. Of course not. Okay.

*The manager hangs up the phone and rubs his eyes.*

*The image returns to the zero-balance message and zooms in slowly.*

### Adam (voice-over)

Lewis didn't think it was safe to send me the file, for obvious reasons, so this is what he was bringing out to the hangar when it all went down.

*The image switches to a silent, slow-motion version of Lazlo introducing himself in the hotel room (see VFILE 2637).*

### Adam (voice-over)

Of course, this changed everything. But how much of it was my fault? Had I been blind to what was really happening to us?

### CLOSE VFILE 2644

The following is a transcript of the video shown by Adam Henderson at 05:31 to H. Ganz in Room 214. Transcription and analysis by H. Ganz.

### OPEN VFILE 2645

*Security-camera shots from the hangar show our own agents entering the facility and conducting a preliminary search.*

#### Adam (voice-over)
We got some unexpected visitors at the hangar. Aren't security cameras fun? Gun on top of the wrist, flashlights on . . . Nice form!

*Two agents approach a locked office.*

#### Adam (voice-over)
Oh, this is great! This is Zara's office. There he goes. Leans back . . . door's open! I bet the main reason these guys signed up for this job is because they love kicking down doors.

*The same two agents are seen from a high angle, guns drawn, deciding to split up.*

### Adam (voice-over)

You'd think they would have figured out by now that there's nobody home. But maybe the thing they like even better than kicking down doors is walking around with their guns drawn.

*Agent Ganz is seen entering suspect Adam's work area, referred to by the suspects as the Vault.*

### Adam (voice-over)

Even though it's creepy having people go through your stuff, this is still my favorite part.

*Agent Ganz takes a call and is joined by the other two agents.*

### Adam (voice-over)

It's so cool the way everyone stands around, taking phone calls, staring at all this equipment, with absolutely no idea that I'm watching them. . . .

## CLOSE VFILE 2645

The following is a transcript of the video shown by Adam Henderson at 05:56 to H. Ganz in Room 214. Transcription and analysis by H. Ganz.

## OPEN VFILE 2646

*A degraded image, possibly shot in the hotel room used by suspects Zara and Lazlo, but apparently exposed in such a way as to make identification impossible. The voices have been altered as well. Two people, one seated, one standing, appear to be addressing the camera.*

### Male speaker

Well, we have our first bad choice by our team of trackers. By disabling the red button, no one gets what they've worked for.

*A process called "enhance video & audio" appears to be activated; both the image and the audio begin to clear up until suspects Zara (seated) and Lazlo (standing) can be identified conclusively. Zara is subdued, staring down at her lap.*

### Lazlo

Everybody loses, but it's the four of you who stand to lose the most. You will lose your freedom, your future.

### Zara

You should know that all the evidence still points to the four of you.

### Lazlo

Would it be a fair trade, you getting things back working again in exchange for us wiping out all this evidence? Maybe not fair, but . . . acceptable.

### Zara

You have to understand, it was never our intention —

### Lazlo (interrupting)

Stick to what's important. There *is* no decision to make. We *will* press the button, and everybody gets what they want.

### Zara

I think we should mention that the whole thing about the Internet shutting down? It's an urban legend, just a myth. What the red button really does is create a sort of digital tornado while we move things around and make things disappear.

### Lazlo

Like who opened the banks, who opened the intel? All these things you've done? There'll be no trail. I know you're the one who disabled it. You're the only one who can put it back together. So we must meet.

**(to Zara)**

Tell him the arrangement.

### Zara

It's public, but yet we can do it all out in the open. We'll give you the Raymond device . . .

*She holds up an object a little larger than a USB flash drive.*

### Zara

. . . and you can make everything work like it's supposed to. We'll have a laptop. We'll activate it right then and there, and we can make sure everything goes according to plan.

### Lazlo

She's, uh, leaving something out, which is that, uh, this fulfills her contract with me. She's free to go after we're done. Maybe you, uh, would want her on your team? Of course, uh, it would be up to you.

### Zara

We'll meet you at the fairgrounds, ten P.M., the bench in front of the Ferris wheel. Keep it simple. Don't try to complicate this . . .

*The image returns to its dark and shadowy original appearance, and the voice-changer is back on.*

**Zara**

. . . Okay?

**CLOSE VFILE 2646**

The following is a transcript of the video shown by Adam Henderson at 06:25 to H. Ganz in Room 214. Transcription and analysis by H. Ganz.

### OPEN VFILE 2647

*A layout of the fairgrounds appears, showing the locations of the Ferris wheel, the carousel, the Tilt-a-Whirl, the midway, the zigzag, the haunted house, and the mirror maze. As Adam describes locations, colored locators appear over them.*

#### Adam (voice-over)

So this was the best plan we could come up with in the time we had. I waited for Lazlo on the bench in front of the Ferris wheel, Lewis had the bird's-eye view up top, Finn found a spot over to my right, and Emily was on my left. I know Zara warned me not to make this complicated, but the way I saw it, it was a little late for that.

*The image switches to surveillance footage from the Belinksi, showing Lazlo making his way through the midway.*

**Finn (offscreen)**

Got him! Heading your way, Adam.

**Adam (voice-over)**

Finn spotted him first.

*In the next sequence, the activities are covered by four different cameras: the Belinski, operated by Finn on one side; the Trinity, operated by Emily on the opposite side; the Deckard, operated by Lewis from above; and a small black-and-white camera, apparently located on Adam's backpack strap, operated by Adam.*

*Lazlo joins Adam on the bench and places a portable computer on his lap. Neither suspect looks at each other. To a casual observer, they might be strangers.*

**Adam**

I want to see Zara.

**Lazlo**

I thought you might. Have one of your team take a look at the house of mirrors.

**Adam (voice-over)**

And there goes the element of surprise. I should have known there would be no hiding from them.

*Adam places his hand on his Bluetooth headset.*

**Adam**

Lewis. What do you see?

*The image switches to the Deckard, scanning for the mirror maze, and stops on a line of people, including Zara.*

**Lewis (offscreen)**

She's last in a line of three.

*Lazlo opens the laptop, takes the Raymond device out of his pocket, and places it on the bench between them.*

**Adam (voice-over)**

He handed me the Raymond device, and I thought, *Okay, this is either going to work, or we're toast.*

*Adam removes a small screwdriver from a pocket and begins disassembling the Raymond device.*

**Lazlo**

Tell me, how do you know for certain you can put that thing back together again the right way?

**Adam**

Photographic memory.

*Adam passes the device back to Lazlo, who inserts it in a port on the side of the laptop.*

**Lazlo**

No more tricks, now. This better work.

**Adam**

It should.

**Adam (voice-over)**

We couldn't pick up a signal from his laptop. He must have had some kind of jamming device installed since the meeting at the hotel.

*Lazlo appears to be testing the Raymond device.*

**Adam (voice-over)**

I don't think time has ever moved more slowly than this. I thought for sure he could tell what I'd done.

*The image switches to Lewis in the Ferris wheel.*

**Lewis**

Adam, see if your mini-cam can pick up his screen.

*Adam adjusts the camera discreetly.*

**Adam (voice-over)**

I tried to aim the mini-cam on my shoulder strap, but the reflection on his screen was too bright.

*The image switches to the shot from Adam's mini-cam. It's impossible to see anything on the screen.*

### Lazlo

Okay. You go that way, I go this way. We will never see each other again. Understood?

### Adam

Can I ask you something? Is Zara really free to go?

### Lazlo

We've talked enough.

*Lazlo looks up in the direction of Lewis before taking off.*

### Adam

Don't lose him.

### Adam (voice-over)

That's when the game of cat and mouse kicked into high gear.

*The image switches from camera to camera, following Adam's narration.*

#### Adam (voice-over)

Emily was closest, and had him for a while . . . then Finn picked him up from farther back, but lost him. Then Emily found him again in the midway . . .

*Emily appears in frame for a moment. . . .*

#### Emily

I lost him!

#### Adam (voice-over)

. . . and Finn got the last frames of him before he vanished into thin air.

#### Finn

Me too.

*After a brief shot of Finn, the Deckard shows Zara entering an amusement ride.*

#### Adam (voice-over)

Then Lewis broke in. . . .

#### Lewis

Zara just went into the mirror maze!

#### Adam

Finn! Emily! Mirror maze, now! Lewis, cover us from up top!

*Finn, Emily, and Adam are seen running toward the mirror maze.*

### Adam

Emily, stay out here and keep your eyes open!

### Emily

I'm on it!

*From the Belinski following close behind, Adam is seen entering the mirror maze. The reflections make it difficult to tell exactly what is happening, but they appear to be progressing through the maze.*

*They emerge from the darkness at what appears to be a rear exit behind the mirror maze.*

### Finn (offscreen)

Don't tell me we lost her.

### Adam

That's what it looks like.

### Adam (voice-over)

By the time we got through the mirror maze and out the back, she was gone. But there was one more surprise waiting for us.

*Finn is shooting with the Belinski from the doorway as Adam descends the stairs to what looks like a parking area for fair personnel. Adam turns and sees something off camera.*

### Adam

Agent Ganz.

*Finn pans the camera over and Agent Ganz appears in frame.*

### Agent Ganz

Time's up, gentlemen. It's time we had a conversation downtown.

### Adam (voice-over)

Lazlo and Zara had written the song, and we had danced to their tune. . . .

*Image switches to a view from the top of the Ferris wheel.*

### Adam (voice-over)

I felt like a puppet on a string. Our only hope was that my programming skills would turn out to be the one thing these puppet masters couldn't control — or predict.

### CLOSE VFILE 2647

# APPENDIX T

The following is a transcript of the video shown by Adam Henderson at 06:59 to H. Ganz in Room 214. Transcription and analysis by H. Ganz.

### OPEN VFILE 2648

*An image appears, or rather many images appear, of suspect Zara. It seems that many layers of cloaking processes have been used on this video, to prevent identification of the source of the feed or examination of any background noise to determine location.*

*Each sentence is its own segment of video, perhaps as a further step to avoid tracing. It appears that the sentences have been reordered and cut up, that they are not in the order originally recorded.*

#### Zara

Lazlo was all about the money, and it cost him. I can never forgive myself. Bravo for me. The digital world has a dark side. I've tried to stop it. You leave me alone, and I'll leave you alone. Stop trying to find me. Stop trying to find me. Stop trying to find me. Technology's funny that way, don't you think? An appetite for destruction. Don't try to find me. Goodbye, Adam Henderson.

*The image of Zara freezes, but the background noise of digital feedback grows in volume and complexity until the whole image goes black.*

**CLOSE VFILE 2648**

# TRACKERS CREDITS

## CAST

| | |
|---|---|
| Adam | James Murray |
| Zara | Morgan Hopper |
| Finn | Urijah Sailes |
| Emily | Chloe Danielson |
| Lewis | John Shaw |
| Lazlo | Eric Derovanessian |
| Ganz | Nelita Davamony-Crawford |
| Hotel Clerk | Cari Wilton |
| Bank Manager | Bill Gilbert |
| FBI Agents | Brom Glidden |
| | Lance Ivy |

## CREW

| | |
|---|---|
| Director | Jeffrey Townsend |
| Writer / Producer | Patrick Carman |
| Associate Producer | Alex English |
| Director of Photography | Brandon Lehman |
| Art Director | Jason Daub |
| Video Editors | Jason Daub |
| | Jeffrey Townsend |
| Assistant Director | Chris Cresci |
| Book Editor | David Levithan |
| Assistant Editor | Gregory Rutty |
| Production Editor | Joy Simpkins |
| Book Design | Christopher Stengel |

| | |
|---|---|
| Designer / Web Developer | Joshua Pease |
| 3-D Models | Straightface Studios / Don Lange |
| Prop Design | Luke Chilson |
| Prop Fabrication | Victor Trejo |
| Hair / Makeup Consultant | Amy Vories |
| Hair / Makeup / Wardrobe Supervisor | Darcy Sturges |
| Hair / Makeup / Wardrobe Assistant | Shane Wood |
| Production Consultants | Sarah Koenigsberg |
| | Amber Larsen |
| Casting Associates | Lindsey Daub |
| | Jennifer Elkington |
| | Tiffany Talent / Tanya Tiffany |
| | Cari Wilton |
| Production Assistants | Amanda Hamilton |
| | Anna Hinz |
| | Elizabeth Shaw |
| Chaperones / Transportation | Jimmy Murray |
| | Theresa Sailes |
| Hospitality | Karen Carman |
| | Patrice Townsend |
| Vehicles | Ford of Walla Walla / Kirk Williams |
| Catering | Graze / John Lastoskie |
| Insurance | State Farm / Liz Conover |

## SPECIAL THANKS

Alan Ketelson and Sonia Schmitt
Banner Bank (Doug Bayne)
Davis Shows (Pat, Geraldine, and Manny Davis)
Exemplar Real Estate (Barb Whatley)
Marcus Whitman Hotel (Shanna Hatfield and Kris Garten)

Mason Helms and Kenneth Butler
Merchants Ltd. (Bob Austin)
Port of Walla Walla (Paul Gerola)
Walla Walla Police Department
Walla Walla University (Jerry Hartman)

For more missions, go to
www.trackersbook.com

# CATCH THE
# TRACKERS

**THE CHALLENGE:** To catch a mastermind cyber thief who operates under the name Shantorian.

**THE TEAM:** Four young Trackers who know the ins and outs of finding someone . . . and not being caught.

**THE TRAP:** Sometimes your friends can turn out to be enemies, and nobody can truly be trusted.

**THE HUNT:** Shantorian must be found, or the Trackers will be blamed for all the damage he has done.

>>>>>>>>>>>>>> **READ THE BOOK** <<<<<<<<<<<<<<
Follow the Trackers as they try to clear their names.

>>>>>>>>>>>>>> **WATCH THE VIDEOS** <<<<<<<<<<<<<<
Click on the links within the book to witness the action.

>>>>>>>>>>>>>> **BREAK THE CODES** <<<<<<<<<<<<<<
Test your code-breaking skills at www.trackersbook.com

Christopher Stengel

...tion is available for distribution only through the school market.

■SCHOLASTIC
www.scholastic.com

9 780545 414555